AIRSHIP 27 PRODUCTIONS

Dan Fowler: G-Man Volume 3

"The Bloody Murdock Brothers" ©2020 Whit Howland
"Dead Man Shooting" ©2020 Gene Moyers
"The Mask of Mesud" ©2020 Aaron Powers
"Family Afoul" ©2020 Fred Adams Jr.

Edited by Ron Fortier
Associate Editor: Michael Housel

Cover illustration ©2020 Chris Rawding
Interior illustrations ©2020 Kevin Paul Shaw Broden
Production and design by Rob Davis
Marketing management by Michael Vance

Published by
Airship 27 Productions
www.airship27hangar.com

ISBN: 978-1-946183-88-0

Printed in the United States of America

10 9 8 7 6 5 4 3 2 1

Dan Fowler
G-Man
Volume Three
Table of Contents

THE BLOODY MURDOCK BROTHERS

By Whit Howland

The old men outside of McClatchy's Barber Shop were immune to the smell of greasy burgers and fries wafting through the diner doorway. They ignored the sound of scraping cans tied to the back of the little boy's scooter as he pushed his way past them down the sidewalk. They sat out front in wicker chairs under the candy cane pole and enjoyed the gentle breeze that carried the sound of church bells and blew through the Cottonwoods lining Main Street. One of the men sipped on a bottle of grape soda and gazed across the boulevard at Plowmen's Bank, as if he was staring right through to the prairie beyond. The other two sat hunched over a game of checkers.

Pretty soon farmers would park their trucks in front of the restaurant. They'd hitch up their overalls, walk in, and plant themselves on one of the stools for a hearty lunch that would tide them over until sundown. All in all, it was a somnolent afternoon in Fairview, Kansas—somnolent until the bank's plate glass window exploded.

Shards of glass rained onto the street. Those on the sidewalk scurried for the meager cover of storefront awnings. Some sought refuge under cars. Others, thinking they could outrun the glass, ran across the thoroughfare.

The old men knocked over their chairs and scurried through the door into the barber shop. When safely inside, the owner locked the door and flipped the sign around from open to "Closed".

Through the bank's window sailed one man clad in a gray pinstripe suit with a bandana across his face. Miraculously, his fedora was still snugly pulled low on his forehead. The man in flight was none other than the infamous and reprehensible Harold Murdock, the oldest of the fearsome, homicidal duo, the bloody Murdock Brothers. Following close behind him, was his equally formidable twin, Rory Murdock.

They'd be carbon copies except Harold had a nasty scar on his cheek. He sported it like a badge of honor. On the other hand, Rory had gone through his dastardly life without a scratch on his movie star face.

The two landed hard on their sides in the middle of the street. Harold was the first to get up and point his .45 into the blown-out window and squeeze off a couple rounds. Rory followed suit by firing two more shots. Both jumped behind a black De Soto and kept shooting into the bank at their unknown opponent. They ducked when return bullets shattered the driver's side mirror.

"Where's the car?" Rory demanded, as he slid another magazine into the handle of his gun.

"It'll be here!" Harold shouted while getting off another shot. Rory brushed along the side of the car and looked into the bank's window. To his glee he saw the security guard poke his head out from behind the tattered curtain. The bank robber wasted no time in shooting the guard's hat off before he put another bullet in his chest. The guard fell over the ledge and onto the sidewalk.

"Goddamn it, I hate it when you do that! Just shoot the sap!" Harold scolded.

"And miss out on the fun?" Rory replied, then war whooped and shot again. By now two other gang members came bursting through the door still blasting. They headed for the cover of a nearby car.

"I thought you yahoos were dead!" Rory shouted.

"Woulda been if you hadn't plugged that security guard," said Bob Chambers, a muscled hood in an ill-fitting gray suit.

"Yeah, imagine that, the old coot and his cohorts had shotguns. We shoulda went in there with choppers!" yelled Mason, a golden-haired youth, also wearing a suit a size too big.

"Didn't count on needing them for a dirt water bank. Where's that damned car!" Rory yelled, returning more fire.

Before Harold had time to respond, a gleaming yellow Packard with bone whitewall tires rushed around the corner. It left a year's worth of smoking rubber on the pavement as it sped toward the crew. The driver's side window rolled down, and a thick hairy arm poked out with a revolver and shot into the air. The four men rushed over to it while shooting back at the bank, and then jumped on the running boards.

The blare of multiple sirens cut through the air. Both Rory and Harold saw a phalanx of police cars coming toward them. The group of vehicles represented all three jurisdictions: State, County and Municipal. They stopped a couple feet in front of the Packard.

Several brawny flatfoots bearing stony expressions exited the vehicles and formed a column. All of them were armed with either a shot gun or BAR rifle. A red-faced, bull-necked sergeant, dressed in uniform blues and a snappy hat, stepped out in front. He placed a megaphone to his lips.

"Give it up, Murdocks. We got you surrounded!"

The driver's side back window of the Packard opened, and the passenger discreetly handed the gang Tommy guns.

"I mean it, you're no match for us even with the heaters!" the sergeant shouted.

Harold gripped his Thompson and squeezed the trigger. "Eat lead, coppers!" The gun jumped around in his arms like a Mexican jumping bean. As the car backed up, Rory and Harold held on while firing, but the remaining two ran across the street and ducked behind cars.

The lawmen started fanning out on the street as the two other robbers chattered away with their heaters. They managed to drop a few cops in a hail of gunfire, but they were greeted by a volley of bullets that perforated the automobile they used for cover.

While the cops kept them busy dodging gunfire, the Packard did a screeching bootleg and turned the corner onto a side street heading out of town. It didn't get too far before it slid to a stop in front of another black and white Packard prowl car. Its cherry-colored beacon winked derisively at the two brothers, while the siren screeched like a hawk closing in on some hapless prey.

The doors swung open on either side and two bulls jumped out and took cover behind door of the car. With their pistols fixed on Harold and Rory, they fired. The bullets brushed by the two criminals' ears causing them to launch from their getaway car running boards. Rory and Harold squeezed their triggers and let loose another volley of bullets, popping holes into every inch of the police car. When Rory smelled gas and saw an amber river inching its way toward them, he made a quick motion to stop shooting.

In a flash of satanic inspiration, Rory whipped out his Zippo. The policemen kept firing but somehow the bullets seemed to go right through the brothers. The gunfire drowned out the familiar clicking of the Zippo when the younger brother flipped the top on the lighter and sparked a flame. He pulled out a cigarette, lit it, puffed, and then flicked it onto the gas trail now nipping at the toe of his Florsheim shoe. The gas ignited, and the fire danced, snaking its way toward the cop car. The two officers tried to flee, but it was too late!

The vehicle caught fire and went up like a pile of dry leaves. Before it had a chance to explode, the bullet ridden yellow Packard backed up, did a one eighty, and left the scene. As it sped away, the robbers heard a *whoosh,* then a *boom* as the other automobile was destroyed. Both Murdocks cackled with maniacal glee ignoring the pyrotechnics behind them.

When the gangsters turned the corner, they were met with a blinding barrage of bullets. Again, a fallen angel was on the side of the Murdocks as the rounds tore through their suits like fiery lead moths but missing them. The car did not fare as well. Its windshield shattered, more bullets pockmarked its frame, and made Swiss cheese out of the occupants inside.

The brothers and the driver scurried for the cover of a Model T. As everyone tensely slipped fresh drums onto their machine guns, bullets exploded all around them.

"Surrender now! You don't know what you're up against!" the sergeant harangued through the bullhorn.

Harold took a deep cleansing breath. "Okay, you apes, are you ready to buck out of here blasting?!"

Rory and the driver nodded.

"We make a break for that blue Oldsmobile across the street!" Harold instructed as he looked over at the vehicle.

Harold led the way, dropping another lawman with two short bursts. The other two took cover behind him firing blindly as they all headed for the car.

With the butt of his gun, Rory smashed the driver's side window, only to see the glass scatter over the back of the driver slouched in a fetal position in the driver's seat.

"Well hot digity, look what we got here!" the brother exclaimed as he manhandled the guy out of the car, "Give me your keys, or you'll be pluckin' a harp!"

The terrified man fumbled for his keys and dropped them on the ground. Rory, in disgust, threw the man aside, and with the toe of his pointed shoe, flipped the keys into the air and reached out and snatched them. He slid in and fired up the engine.

Following the sound of gunfire, Bob Chambers and Mason crept their way up to the Oldsmobile firing cover shots as they went. Rory backed the car closer to them.

"Come on, let's go before we stop being so lucky!" Rory shouted.

Harold jumped in beside his brother. Chambers, and Dexter, the driver, scrambled into the back seat. As Mason was getting in on the other side, he felt a burning sensation in his stomach. A crimson rose in full bloom appeared on his white dress shirt. He stared at it in disbelief. Bob Chambers reached over and pulled him into the car. The boy's face pressed the leather of the backseats.

The robbers turned and sped out of town in the opposite direction, even though Mason was only half in the car. The metal heels on his shoes made sparks on the pavement.

"How many do you think are in there with Pardue?" Kendall asked the man standing next to him. Kendall was an FBI agent and the gent was none other than Dan Fowler, renowned G-Man.

Fowler said nothing as he looked through the binoculars pressed to his bronzed face. His broad shoulders tensed, and his sturdy jaw constricted as he watched a cook dumping a bag of trash into the garbage can. The man was jittery.

"You think they sense something's up?" asked another agent.

"Any criminal worth his salt is always paranoid," Fowler said as he pulled the glasses away, folded them and stuffed them into his navy-blue suit.

Kendall with his dashing good looks smiled at his partner. The two other agents stood in silence staring down at the honky-tonk.

"All right, time to get this done. Kendall and I will go through the front. You two cover the back. Keep your gats handy because there is sure to be gunplay."

The joint resembled an indoor mountain hideaway. Plush green plants filled the room floor to ceiling, and a tree trunk planted in the middle of the floor looked like Jack's beanstalk. There were plastic birds on the trees making metallic chirping sounds. A tuxedoed bartender stood behind a mahogany counter and was ready to serve the men seated at the felt table in the middle of the floor. The big man in the center with a bellowing voice held court. His shoulders looked as if they would burst out of his shiny suit. This should have been Buster Pardue, but it wasn't.

Pardue was the man seated at the end of the bar. A pyramid of shot glasses stood in front of him. His lanky body formed an "S" as he hunched over the counter. He was hitting it pretty hard, but he always did when he was thinking about his next heist. Money was getting lean and the crew needed a big score. So, he drank and sweated over the details.

"Hey Boss, come on over and have some fun!" the hulk called over to him. Buster Pardue shot his compadre an annoyed look. "I'm busy thinking!"

"Aw shucks, you worry too much!" replied the big man.

Buster Pardue drained another tiny glass. "You wanna keep blowing your nose through silk hankies, you'll leave me to my thoughts!"

The large gent shrugged and despite his big mitts that passed for hands, dealt out more cards with expert grace. Before placing his hands on his temples, Pardue looked on at the others and then went back to figuring all the angles of the next job.

It was to be another bank heist. As always, the scheme had been sold to him as a simple in and out. But it never was that. Pardue hadn't known a job where there wasn't a glitch. Someone always tipped someone off and before you knew it, the cops were on you like a pack of feral dogs, guns blazing. So that's why Buster Pardue always sweated. He had a plan A, B and C for any eventuality.

Pardue prided himself in being a thinking man's hood, and he always figured that robbing banks and armored shipments was just a stopgap until he could work his way into some safer rackets. But until then he was stuck as the boss of a stick-up crew. Right now, that was okay.

As he was lost in his thoughts, he faintly heard the scratch of a record needle. Some tinny jazz filled the room. As he was about to turn and tell the barkeep to shut it off, *Boom!* The front door blew off its hinges and billowing smoke filled the room and choked out the rest of the gang.

But Pardue was always present and in the moment. As he stood up, he reached for a cloth napkin, and covered his face with one hand and hurled his stool in the direction of the smoke with his other. Then he drew his .45.

His cronies had recovered and were trading fire with the agents who emerged from the gray sulfuric cloud.

Dan Fowler was in front of the posse with his gun blazing as he made for the cover of the counter.

When Pardue spied Fowler, he thought it best to run for the exit. So, like a gazelle, he dashed to the kitchen. Fowler vaulted from his sanctuary and took after the gangster. Bullets whistled past him and one tore through the lapel of his blue suit coat. *Damn,* he thought briefly—but only briefly because right now he had to stay focused.

As Dan Fowler raced through the kitchen, he caught a fleeting glimpse of Pardue vanishing through the side exit. As he tried to pursue the crook, a hood in an apron tripped him.

Pardue's lungs felt like they were being stabbed with a red-hot poker, as he ran as fast as he could across the dusty prairie. When he figured he was in the clear, he slowed to a jog. Turning to glance behind him he ran into the stiff blue-coated arm of Dan Fowler, landing with a *thud* on the hard earth.

"Your lucky streak's over, Pardue!" Fowler said as he stepped on the man's stomach.

"Where'd you come from?" Pardue asked in disgust. Fowler just smiled as though he had swallowed a canary.

"Hold on a little longer, buckaroo, we are almost to the hospital," Chambers said.

Bloody handprints stained the backseats and windows. Heel prints covered the back of the front seat. Blood was on the men's suits. Blood was everywhere. Rory had just about enough. What he could not stand more than the blood was Mason's caterwauling. The boy flailed about and convulsed, often, hitting Rory and Harold in the head. If Bob Chambers had not been holding him down, Rory would have turned around and put one right through the young criminal's forehead, ending everyone's suffering.

"I know you and the boy are close, but you're going to have to do a better job of shuttin' him up," said Harold.

Chambers brushed back the young man's hair in an attempt to be a comforting presence. This seemed to mollify Mason. The older man helped matters even more by giving the boy a leather belt to bite down on. Mason chomped down hard on it.

"That's much better," Bob Chambers remarked.

As Harold drove pell-mell away from the town, the car lurched left and right.

"Don't worry, we'll be at the doctor's office soon enough!"

Both Harold and Rory grinned wickedly at each other, as they drove onto a wooded trail. Eventually, the car skidded to a halt. Mason whimpered but kept sucking and slurping loudly on the belt. Harold turned to Chambers and nodded his head.

The burly gangster sighed and opened the door and gently herded Mason out of the car. He cradled the boy in his big arms. Both Rory and Harold watched through the windshield as the lumbering Chambers carried the boy into the woods.

"Is the doc's…" Mason gurgled. The more seasoned hood just shushed him. Pretty soon the two were swallowed up in the trees. Everyone in the car waited, and then it came; two shots that echoed through the trees—the mercy killing.

Leather-bound law books lined the wall from ceiling to floor. It was an impressive library. The big picture window looked out on the mall in Washington, DC. The Director, a silver haired, broad-shouldered man sat at his desk. With his hat in his hand, Dan Fowler stood before him.

"Pardue was a tough assignment, but that's why you were picked," said the Director.

"We knew if we kept at it, eventually he'd make a mistake, and he did," Fowler replied.

The Director raised his eyebrows and nodded in acknowledgement. He reached into a drawer, pulled out a manila folder, and handed it to the FBI agent. Fowler opened it.

"We got another one for you. Two bad brothers that are cutting a bloody swath across the plains and parts of Texas."

"I've heard of these scalawags and was wondering when I would get a crack at them," Fowler said, his head buried in the folder.

"Well, wonder no more! They are very active so I'm sure you will pick up their scent pretty quickly."

"Should I take Kendall and Sally?" Dan Fowler asked.

"Absolutely!" the Director exclaimed.

As he walked down the hall, Dan Fowler's heels clacked on the linoleum. He hadn't gone far when he heard a familiar voice.

"Where are you off to now?"

Fowler stopped and turned to see Sally Vane, a very attractive agent, standing there. Vane had often assisted Fowler on cases and had proven very capable when things got heavy. Besides Kendall, there wasn't anyone he'd rather have by his side than Sally Vane, and, she felt the same way about him.

"The Chief has put us on the Murdock Brothers case."

"I have heard about them—a real bad bunch," she replied.

He nodded in agreement, then raised his eyebrows as if he had an inspiration. "Say, I am going to talk to Buster Pardue down in the holding pen, to see what he knows about the Murdocks. Care to join me?"

"Why, I would be delighted!" she replied with a coy smile.

Dan Fowler smiled as well and kept walking, Sally Vane following after him.

"Whaddya want, Copper? Can't you see I'm busy?"

Fowler gripped the bars firmly. He pushed himself back from the jail cell, loosened his tie and took off his jacket. Buster Pardue, experienced in the ways of aggression, sensed Fowler's demeanor and opened his eyes. He saw the jailer opening the cell door and Dan Fowler purposefully walking in. Pardue held up his hands.

"You ain't thinking about getting rough with me are you, Copper?" The jail cell door clanged shut and Fowler cracked his knuckles.

"You play nice and answer a few questions, then no rough stuff will be necessary," Fowler replied.

Vane, who was standing against the institutional gray wall, stepped forward, a look of concern plastered on her face.

Pardue got up from the bed, slinked over to the corner and crouched into a defensive fighter's stance.

"I ain't no pushover, flatfoot. You swing on me, I'll swing back!"

The agent pulled his pistol out of his rig and calmly emptied the cylinder, letting the bullets fall to the floor. He pointed the gun at Buster.

"Dan, what are you are doing! Are you crazy?" Vane shrieked.

Fowler ignored her, continuing to point the revolver at Pardue. "Now, Buster, what can you tell me about the Murdock Brothers?"

"Ha! I know that gun ain't loaded, so bite my shorts, G-Man!"

"I guess you're not much of a gambler, so I'm thinking you don't play too many games of chance."

"If this is Russian Roulette, then I played that one before!" Pardue replied.

"Not my kind," Fowler replied, grinning.

Although Pardue could feel the sweat in his armpits, he donned his best poker face. "Yeah, yeah Copper, I've played 'em all."

"But probably not this one," Fowler said as he squeezed the trigger. A bullet nearly winged the gangster's ear. Pardue lurched back, surprised, but he recovered quickly, leering at the agent.

Meanwhile Sally Vane stood back from the cell door, shuddering. Fowler continued to point the pistol at Pardue. This time he aimed for his knee cap.

"Ha! You don't have any more bullets!" Pardue said. Fowler shrugged and squeezed the trigger. *Click.*

This was Pardue's cue to lunge for the agent. Fowler squeezed off another shot which reverberated throughout the cell. The bullet grazed the hood's collar and paralyzed him with shock.

"Dan!" Vane screamed.

Fowler took a cleansing breath. "This ends if you tell me what I want. What do you know about the Murdock Brothers?"

Pardue wheezed as he gulped for air. "I don't know nothin! 'Sides if I did, I wouldn't tell you!"

The hood was scared, but his reputation and survival depended on being a tough nut to crack.

Fowler pointed at his chest and squeezed the trigger again. *Click!*

"Dan, stop! You'll kill him!" Sally Vane pleaded as she pounded the bars.

Pardue began to twitch. Vane screamed again. Fowler pointed the gun just above the perp's head and fired. Pardue closed his eyes, bracing for what was to come. *Click.*

"You won't break me, Copper! You won't!" Pardue hissed through ragged breaths.

"I'm gonna ask you again, what do you know about the Murdock Brothers!"

"You know that if I sing, I'm dead in the big house! So, I'll take my chances!"

Fowler popped three more bullets into the cylinder and then spun it. Pardue tried another weak pass at the G-Man. Fowler reached out and kicked him against the wall, knocking the wind out of him as he hit the concrete.

"I've got plenty of bullets, Buster. We can do this all night. Up to you!" Fowler said twirling his gun.

Drawing in another defiant breath, Pardue just stood there staring saucer-eyed at the agent. Dan Fowler knowing his tactics were achieving his goal, and that it was time to enact the final stages of the plan, pointed his pistol again at Pardue.

The crook, this time pretty sure that it would be another miss, stood straight and did his best to look tough. Dan Fowler aimed the gun at the front of his pants and squeezed the trigger. The shot popped into the wall just between the man's legs. Pardue lost all control. Tears streamed down his face and he mumbled uncontrollably. Fowler holstered his pistol, lit a cigarette and took a puff.

"Take your time, Pardue. Spill the beans. All of them."

Fowler mopped his face with a handkerchief and took in the cool air thrown around by the ceiling fan. Sally Vane came up the stairs shortly after him. Fowler reached for a cup, poured her some coffee and handed it to her.

"Wow, I thought we were just going to do a standard 'Mutt and Jeff'. You know, where I bat my eyes and talk to him in soothing tones after you had softened him up."

"We were going to do that, but he just broke down a lot faster than I expected him to."

Vane laughed. "Yeah, that surprised me, too. So, what do you think? Anything we can use?"

Dan Fowler paused and thought for a moment. "The fact that they like the night spots is significant. Means they like to throw money around. And it also indicates that this is one time where their guard is down."

A large band played a swing number. They were fifteen strong packed on a small stage. Trumpeters, trombones and sax players. Two plucked weathered stand-up basses, while another beat on some battered drums.

The crowd danced as if there was no tomorrow. Most did the jitterbug. Some executed it better than others. Ties flapped in the breeze. Shoes scuffed the floor. There were zoot suits, sailors in their ice cream-colored uniforms, farm boys with checkered sleeves rolled up to reveal red arms, and the Murdock Brothers.

Rory twirled a dame as she did a pirouette, all the while puffing on a cigarette that dangled limply from his mouth. Harold, with his tie around his head, crowed like a rooster, grabbed his girl and spun her madly. The rest of the crew hung back, sitting at a table. Dexter swilled beer, while Bob Chambers pulled on the hard stuff.

"We shut the place down, didn't we boys!"

"Work hard. Play hard. That's the Murdock way," Harold said, taking a gulp of bonded whiskey. Rory reached out his hand and Harold passed the bottle his way.

"That's some good hooch!" Rory said taking a healthy drink.

"So, what's the next job?" Chambers asked, lighting another rolled cigarette, then putting it in his mouth and puffing on it.

The room smelled like stale smoke. The gang had rented the finest suite in the joint. It had a small sitting area with a couch and chairs, and a good-sized coffee table that the guys were comfortably resting their feet on.

"Don't know," said Harold, "It ain't much of a priority now."

"Yeah, 'sides, we just got finished with the last one!" Rory added.

Dexter got up off the sofa and headed for the door.

"Whatsa matter, we chopped liver, too good for us?" Rory slurred.

"Just going out for some air. My head hurts," Dexter responded.

This caused a cacophony of catcalls from the others.

"Poor wittle baby. His head hurts?" Rory sneered.

"Want some aspirin?" Chambers asked.

"No, thanks," Dexter said. "Just need some air."

Rory got up and blocked his way. "You ain't going nowhere."

Dexter recoiled as the blast of the brother's dragon and booze breath hit his face.

"Rory!"

Rory turned to the sound of his brother's voice. "Let 'em go, if he wants to!"

The other Murdock smirked at Dexter as he stepped out of the way. "Fine, we don't like your company anyway." The gangster then hiccupped. Harold looked up at the paint-chipped ceiling, then pulled out a pack of cigarettes and shook one out.

"What time is it?" Bob asked.

"Don't know, it's definitely past midnight," Harold responded, popping the cigarette in his mouth and lighting it. He blew smoke out of his nose and then pulled back the shabby, faded, red-velvet curtain.

Outside a streetlamp flickered and then went out. Harold looked to the left and saw the orange glow of another tobacco stick. Past that he saw the outlines of dark figures moving swiftly across the street. He took another

"We shut the place down, didn't we boys?"

drag on his cigarette and flicked it across the room.

"All right you apes, grab your gats, 'cause we got company."

"What's up, boss!"

"Bulls," Harold replied pulling his Tommy Gun from its violin case.

"Bulls, how the hell did they find us?" Rory asked.

"Got some ideas, but not sure yet," Harold replied tossing his brother the other machine gun.

Dan Fowler led the other agents up the stairs. Even though they were doing their best to keep quiet, the bowed and rotting wood creaked under their feet. Sally Vane was right behind him. Fowler looked around as he ascended the steps. The space was narrow, and he knew the hallway would be just as confined. He wondered briefly if they should have tried to nab the gang in the street. But it was too late to turn back now. Sure enough, the hallway, with its sickly yellow walls was just as tight. Except for an abandoned maid's cart stocked with all sorts of cleaning supplies, and a metal trash can, it was empty. Dan Fowler's trained mind catalogued the contents of the cart. He also noticed the garbage can was only half full— still heavy, but he and his posse could heft it and throw it if they had to.

Dan Fowler no sooner finished his thought when a shot rang out and a bullet skimmed the air in front of his nose, lodging in the plaster wall. Choking briefly on the dust, he bounded to a doorway across the hall. The rest of the crew followed behind, leapfrogging and taking cover in doorways. The agent motioned for them to stay put.

"Cover me!" he hissed.

With all his might he shouldered open the door causing the wood to split. The faint odor of sweat and perfume hit him when he barged into the room. A blood-curdling female scream greeted him. Glancing over at the bed, he saw a woman sitting upright, using her hands to cover the upper part of her pale body. Next to her was a man with a beer gut and strands of hair pointing out like porcupine quills from his balding head, a chagrined look of shock on his face.

Fowler motioned for both to get up and get in the closet. He then peered through the doorway and another shot echoed down the hall and smashed the far window. He felt relieved that he had agents on the street covering the exits. The gang must have realized their plan. Dan Fowler figured it made better sense for them to shoot their way out the front, rather than to try going down the fire escape, leaving themselves more vulnerable.

Fowler's presence prompted one of the brothers to pop out and squeeze off a few rounds. Fowler ducked back in. He then motioned to Vane across the hallway to take cover, giving her cover fire as she went.

As a volley of shots came her way and clanged into the garbage can, she ran to the nearest door and smashed her way in.

"Let's break for the window!" Bob Chambers suggested.

Harold scoffed, "They got men on the street waiting to pick us off the minute we show our mugs! Our best bet is to blast our way out the front. We'll grab some civilians and use them as shields if we have to."

"That's nuts. There's at least four still in the doorway. It might take a while, but they'll overrun us for sure!"

Rory turned to Chambers in disgust. "Gotta better idea? Spill it!"

Bob Chambers looked out the window. "I'll head down the fire escape, create a diversion. Maybe I can meet up with Dexter on the street. We can plug some flatfoots and double around and get the coppers in the hotel in a pickle. This could give you guys some breathing room to get out the front door. Then we make for the car."

Harold braced himself in the doorway and chattered away with his "Chicago Typewriter." "That doesn't sound like much of a plan to me, but it's your funeral!"

Chambers wasted no time, slinging his weapon over his shoulder. He ran to the window, pried it open and stepped through it.

As he crouched on the fire escape, steamy air enveloped the man's face. The rusty structure rang like a church bell as bullets hit it. The hood knew he had to get to the street fast. Since he knew he wouldn't be able to return fire, he also knew his chances of making it were slim. If he were to stay in that room, they'd all be dead. Half of him wanted to desert Harold and Rory, but he was too loyal—and they still hadn't divided up the loot. So, he had a vested interest in keeping those maniacs alive.

As quickly as he could go, he scrambled down the fire escape. Dawn was beginning to break, and the purple strands of morning were just enough light for his eyes to see what was below. As he descended the steps, he saw agents and police behind cars with their guns pointed upward. More bullets zinging by his head inspired him to make a Hail Mary jump to the pavement.

Stepping on the moveable ladder, he reached for a rung. By the grace of a lesser god, he made his way to the bottom rung and grabbed onto it. Rust flaked in his hand as he gripped it and the ladder rattled as it extended.

Chambers swung outward and hurled himself into the air, almost doing a jackknife as he sailed toward the ground.

Despite doing his best to break the fall, pain vibrated through his body when he landed on his side, colliding with the hood of a car. It was the superhuman adrenaline that kept him going as he brought himself upright and clambered off the car.

Coincidentally, this was a vehicle that an agent covering the street had been hiding behind. The G-Man swung at Bob Chamber's head with the butt of his gun. The rifle glanced off the top of the gangster's crown, but he was still smarting from the fall and didn't feel the full effect of the blow. He responded by grabbing the lapels of the man's jacket as he head-butted him.

The man's head snapped back, with a sharp chop to the agent's neck, Chambers ended the altercation. The man quickly flopped to the street. Normally, the crook would have finished off his foe by bashing his brains in with his gun, but he was pressed for time. Gripping his gun, he swung around and started blasting away at any head that popped up. He kept firing until he heard a *click*.

Without a second thought, he unburdened himself of his spent weapon. He picked up the unconscious agent's gun, resuming fire.

Gray smoke filled the air, and a pile of burning, greasy rags created a wall of fire at the end of the hallway. Even though a handkerchief covered Dan Fowler's face, he still coughed. But the discomfort was worth the tactical advantage they had gained, because now they could get more agents into the hallway and outnumber the perpetrators. Fowler, Sally Vane and the other agents were now zigzagging their way down the corridor. Only occasional fire came from the crooks, but the shots went wild. Because he could hear them hacking, Fowler knew the smoke was affecting the bad guys as well. He only hoped that the innocent people in the building were able to escape by using the fire escapes to safety. Nevertheless, he saw this was the only way to end what was turning out to be a heavy battle.

Machine gun fire came from the direction the agents had entered. The team was caught in a turkey shoot. Fowler fired behind his shoulder and ducked back into another room.

"Damn!" he exclaimed to himself. The whole thing had been a gamble and now it was looking like an error of judgment, and he had only himself to blame.

"What do we do now, Dan?" asked an agent.

"Retreat to my location and stand down," Fowler replied, defeated.

Harold coughed violently and so did Rory. But their mood brightened when they realized that the shooting had stopped.

"Maybe Bob made it?" Rory asked.

Harold shrugged his shoulders and coughed some more. "Search me, but I think it's time for us to cheese it!"

Harold crouched low and went into the hallway. Rory followed close behind, his hand covering his mouth.

"How 'bout another Coke for this lovely young thing here?" Rory asked the counter clerk.

The two brothers were sitting at the lunch counter in a five and dime in Morton, Oklahoma. Beside them sat two young local girls. One was blonde and the other a brunette. Their gingham dresses and ruddy faces showed that they were farm girls. That was okay with the brothers because the more wholesome the dame, the more pliable they were. These women proved to be no exception to that rule. Their wide eyes looked at the brothers as they swapped stories. They blushed every time either Harold or Rory threw money around for their benefit.

"So, what do you fellas do?" asked Rosemary, the blonde.

"We're traveling salesmen," Harold replied.

"Yeah, that's what we are, sales chaps," Rory added.

"You must make a lot of money," said Lucille.

The only time the girls had seen men dress this nice was on Sunday at church. Other than that, all the men in their town wore coveralls, boots and Stetson hats. None of them ever looked as dapper as the "gents" now before them. To the girls, these were the type of men who would take them to fancy restaurants, plays and concerts in some big city, far away from Morton. They were their ticket out of "Smallsville".

"Yeah, we do all right," Rory said.

"You must do more than all right," Rosemary replied sidling closer to Harold, "What do you sell?"

Rory and Harold looked at each other and grinned. Although they were trying to keep a low profile, sometimes the situation was too rich to pass up some fun.

"Uh, we sell cowpoke stuff," said Harold as he snorted into his tie.

"Cowpoke stuff?" asked Lucille.

"Uh, yeah, cowpoke stuff and farm implements." Rory half mumbled and snickered. The girls looked at each other, grinned and shook their heads. The truth was they didn't care what these men did as long as they kept doting on them.

Larry, the bald, paunchy soda-fountain clerk, had worked most of his life in this general store. Larry was a simple man and liked simple things. He saw right and wrong—and that was all there was to it. There was nothing right about these two city slickers. Larry could see it when they entered. He saw it in the smug looks on their faces. He saw it in their swagger. These were men that knew how to get what they wanted by way of force. Larry knew bullies when he saw them. And their last remark was the final straw.

Unable to stand anymore of their shenanigans, he casually reached down and rifled through the pile of Wanted posters he'd collected from police officers who occasionally stopped by to deliver a new bulletin.

There they were! Harold and Rory Murdock! His hands were so sweaty that he wiped them on his dirty apron. The fear and excitement caused him to shake—only he didn't know it. Unfortunately, the brothers did. It was obvious that he was shuddering, as if he just got out of a washtub full of ice cubes.

"Hey, you sick or something?" Harold asked.

"Uh yeah, I, I am getting over a fever!" Larry replied.

"That so!" Rory exclaimed.

Harold took another sip of cherry cola. The girls, not unaware of the shift in mood, glanced at each other. Rosemary started to get up, but Harold clamped a hand on her shoulder pushing her back down on the stool.

"You know, the funny thing is that you were not shaking a few minutes ago, but now you are... and that's bothering me."

"Yeah, it's bothering me too," Rory added.

With his mind revving and racing, Larry held up his hands, trying to slow things down. He wasn't the brightest guy, but he was an expert at making excuses and getting himself out of jams.

"I get nervous. They give me medication for it; I guess I haven't taken it yet today," Larry said.

Harold gave the shopkeeper the once over. Then he shrugged. "Alright, makes sense, but take your peepers off me; staring ain't polite."

"Sorry, sir," Larry said.

"Just don't let it happen again or we'll stiff you on the tip," Rory said, chuckling.

Larry stood there, nervously blinking. It was all he could stand. He felt the back of his neck get hot and the hairs begin to rise. All his life, the town's people and his wife thought him to be ineffectual. With electricity surging through him, he felt it was time to act—to make himself a hero. But how would he do it?

As Larry was mustering the courage do something, Harold wiped his mouth with his pocket square and then jammed it into his coat. He got up, throwing a wad of bills on the counter.

"Well, soda jerk, it's been fun but we gotta get rolling. Be good, and hey… take your meds!"

Rory went into a fit of laughing, so much so that spit flew from his mouth onto Harold's lapel. Harold wiped it off in an exaggerated dignified manner.

"Soda Jerk?" Rory asked, still laughing.

"What! That's what they call 'em, chowderhead. Sack up, and let's go!" Harold ordered.

Both Harold and Rory collected their gals and swaggered out the door. Larry watched them, noticing the nice cut of their suits. He wasn't sure which made him angrier—the way they were acting and treating him, or the fact that he's never been able to wear clothes as nice as theirs. Or, maybe that he would never be with nice young girls such as those.

Whatever it was, it turned into a scorching fireball that rose from his gut to his head, making his eyeballs burn. Unable to stand it anymore, he was ready to bolt out the door. Then, something made him take a deep breath that was just enough to clear his head. So, instead of making a heroic stand, he went over to the phone, picked up the receiver, and dialed.

Crows lined the telephone wires and cawed, serenading Main Street. Across the way, one man held a ladder while the other stood atop and changed the movie title on the marquee of the movie theater.

Like two crazy crowned princes, Harold and Rory walked down the sidewalk.

"So, whadda ya think, toots, like some jewelry?" Harold asked Lucille. The farm girl beamed ear to ear and pulled harder on the hood's shirt sleeve.

"And what about you, butter cup?" Rory asked the blonde who hung on his arm.

"Leaping lizards, that would be great! But there isn't any store around here where you can get nice things," Rosemary replied.

Both Harold and Rory looked at each other and laughed. The ladies looked bewildered. Then Lucille started to pout. Harold patted the woman on the small of the back.

"It's okay, we only laugh because we think life is full of funny things and merriments."

"Yeah, all the world's a joke and we are merely jokers and stuff like that!"

Rosemary in a moment of pragmatism looked at Rory. "But where're you going to get the jewelry?"

Rory chuckled again. "That's what I like, a dame who's all business. We could use a moll like you…"

Harold cleared his throat and caught his brother's attention. When Rory turned to him, his brother gave him the throat-slitting gesture.

"We'll get you some nice shiny jewelry on Park Avenue in New York City. How 'bout that?"

"We'd love to see New York!" Lucille said.

"Then it's settled!" Harold said.

The quartet sauntered down the sidewalk and all was pleasant until the high-pitched whine of a police siren interrupted their placid stroll. Both women could feel Harold and Rory become tense.

"What's the matter? It's only Archie the deputy," Lucille assured them.

"You broads better be cool as cucumbers!" Harold snarled as he nudged his woman along.

"Ouch! You're hurting me!" Lucille pleaded.

"Howdy!" Archie yelled as he exited his prowl car and walked toward the group. Both Harold and Rory pulled their hats low and lowered their eyes. The two women started to fidget. Archie, seemingly unfazed, kept advancing. "So, who are your friends there, ladies?"

Both the hoods continued to avoid the lawman. Archie's smile began to fade, and his eyes narrowed a tiny bit.

"I'm guessing neither of you are from around here. Just visiting?"

"Yeah, something like that, cop…I mean officer," Harold replied.

"Right, we're just taking in the beautiful sights," Rory added. Archie raised his eyebrows and looked around ever so slightly. "Well, I reckon there's a lot of beautiful scenery."

"You bet, officer," Harold replied as he leered at the girl by his side. Archie frowned when he caught the gangster's glance, and his hand reflexively moved toward his holstered gun.

"Say, you fella's mind showing me some ID?"

Rory's hand casually slipped into his pocket. Harold pushed his hat up on his forehead. "There a problem, officer?"

Archie sighed, doing his best to keep the conversation casual. But as hard as he tried, it was plain to see that every muscle in his body was constricting. Still, he did his best in fighting a losing battle to keep up appearances. "Well, I'm sure it's nothing, but we got a telegram from the FBI about two brothers out on a cross country robbing spree."

This time Rory raised his eyebrows. "Really?"

Archie laughed nervously and with his fingers, worried the leather on his holster. As he saw the lawman fiddle with his weapon, Harold started to sweat.

"Not that anyone of that sort would have any interest in *this* little town, and you fellas really don't look like the type. But just the same, we were told to keep on a heightened state of alert. So, if it's no trouble, how about I see your IDs."

"…mind showing me some ID?"

Lucille and Rosemary grew even more uncomfortable. Lucille wrenched herself away from Harold and grabbed Rosemary, pulling the woman to her.

"Come on, Rosemary, we should be getting home."

Before Harold or Rory could protest, the girls started down the block. Rory's blood, which was already simmering, now began to boil. In his squirmy mind, this schlep cost him serious fun and frolic with some willing corn-fed gals.

Everything about this constable made his skin crawl, causing him to turn his back to the man and slowly pull out a glass flask. He jammed a handkerchief into the top and slowly lit the fuse.

"Whenever you're ready, I'll take your ID," Archie said.

"Don't worry, you'll get it," Rory replied. With a cackle, he whipped around and smashed the flask at the officer's feet. Harold roared with laughter as he pulled his flask and added more liquor to the flame. As the flames spread up the Deputy's body, the two hoods quickly moved back. The brothers continued to laugh as Archie screamed and flailed about. They pulled their guns and shot in the air like outlaws in the Old West. The girls screamed and started running for their lives. Still shooting, the brothers turned and ran for the car.

Even though it had been a couple days, both Lucille and Rosemary trembled as they talked to Sally Vane. She was doing her best to be empathetic—in the way only a woman could be to another woman. But, obviously, the memory of the brutal murder of a friend, whom they had known for a lifetime, was too overwhelming for the ladies. True, they were looking to shed their small-town ways—but not like this! They wanted bright lights and the hustle and bustle of big city life. Instead, they had witnessed what bad men could do to other men. It took all of Vane's skill as a trained agent and empathy as a human being to keep these young ladies from slipping inward into their tormented psyches.

Apart from the three women, Dan Fowler and Kendall stood with three other agents and Jack Malone, the town's beefy marshal. Even though Marshal Malone was fat, he was all spit and polish. This was especially true of the tin star on his chest. He took extra care in shining that piece of metal to a brilliant luster. In fact, it shined so bright, Dan Fowler and the other men almost had to shield their eyes from the glare.

"So, whaddya make of all this, Agent Fowler?" Marshal Malone asked.

Fowler motioned to the agent with the camera to snap more photos of the charred body that was before them. He surveyed the scene and the corpse with soft eyes, as he was trained to do. It would be soft eyes that would enable him to see what he needed to see, the telltale signs that would give him more insight into this bad bunch he was pursuing.

Marshal Malone took off his Stetson and put it over his heart as he stared at the body. "Known Archie since he was a young boy. Watched him grow up and play ball. Mentored him all through his law enforcement training. Never dreamed he would go out like this."

"The world is a bad place, and these days one can't escape it, even in a nice small town like this," Kendall replied.

"Especially if you're a cop, I mean we're all one day away from being rubbed out some way or another," the agent with the camera added.

Fowler let the callous comment pass over him as he continued to investigate. Just as he was about to give up, he absently looked down at the tip of his shoe. There it was. The clue!

A poker chip might not mean anything to the average lay person. But to an agent with a nimble mind such as Dan Fowler's, it spoke volumes about where the perps might be headed next. As Fowler studied the gambling artifact, he deduced that they would undoubtedly end up somewhere in Nevada, possibly Las Vegas. Unfortunately, in order to confirm his suspicions, he would have to wait to see where they would strike next.

"Whaddya got, Dan?" Kendall asked.

"Poker chip!"

"Ahh, you think they're headed to Vegas?"

"Could be. In any case, put out an APB in Utah, Arizona and Nevada. I can't be sure, but there's a good chance this bunch will push as far west as they can go."

As it rolled through what should have been Main Street in this dusty ghost town, the car crunched rocks and other debris. And a ghost town it was, with windowless, dilapidated buildings. Its prominent feature was a mill with a water wheel. The river had dried up long ago. The car pulled to a stop, and both Rory and Harold stepped out. Bob Chambers and Dexter followed suit. Rory stretched, exclaiming, "What a jumping burg this is!" Harold sniffed the air.

"Yeah, people just die laughing in this place!" he replied looking over at some bleached human bones.

"It looks like the buzzards and critters picked this place clean," Chambers chimed in.

"I'll bet in the day, this town had a juicy bank," Rory said.

Harold looked around as if he was visualizing the way the place looked when it was populated. He held his hands up framing each building.

"The bank had to have been there," he said. "Over there was the saloon; you can tell by the doorway, big enough for a pair of bat wings."

"So, what are we doing here?" Bob Chambers asked.

As Rory lit a cigarette and eyed two buzzards on the hitching post, Harold continued visualizing how the town had once looked.

"Well, Bob!" Rory said. "It seems we got a ferret among us."

"A ferret?" Chambers asked.

"Yeah, someone who snitches to the cops."

"Oh, I get it, you mean a weasel or a mole."

"Yeah, weasel, mole, ferret… same thing!" Harold said, finally getting down to business.

Chambers and Dexter looked at each other. The muscled hood held out his hands in an open gesture. "Harry, who's the rat? I'll do him myself!"

Harold grinned wickedly. "You'll do him yourself. That's rich. That's exactly what we have in mind." Harold took a long gaze at the ghost town. "You know, this town reminds me of one of those places in the movies where the cowboys draw down on each other in a gunfight."

Dexter began to sweat, and it wasn't because of the heat. Rory circled both Chambers and Dexter like a buzzard waiting for them to die.

"No doubt you two are figuring out what we got in mind," Rory said.

"Boys…!" Bob Chambers pleaded.

"Who you calling boys!" Harold menaced.

Chambers wiped his brow. It wasn't that he feared death. In his line of work, he knew it would come sometime soon. But this didn't mean that his mind didn't spin into preservation mode. The way he saw it, nothing was over until you said it was over, and he meant to explore every option at his disposal. "I'm sorry, gentlemen. I don't know where you're getting that either one of us is a rat; we've been loyal through and through!"

Harold lit a cigarette and blew smoke at the clear sky. As he felt the sun on his face, the prickly heat on his neck indicated he was hot under the collar. He liked Bob. But when he used that tone of voice, the one that sounded as if he was trying to reason with a child, the lug had a way of getting under his skin.

"Well, Bob," Harold said solemnly, "I've been readin' the Bible. Sort of got religion and all that. You know what my favorite story is?"

Bob Chambers stared at his boss with a stony expression.

"The story of Solomon, you know the one where he says to split the baby down the middle. So, I get this idea, why don't we do the same thing here to determine who's the rat?"

Still confused, Chambers and Dexter looked at each other. Rory snickered. Harold removed his hat and reverently put it over his heart.

"In the spirit of religion, we're gonna have a good old fashion gunfight to split the baby down the middle."

Bob Chambers thought about the implication and shook his head. "Not to be contrary, but I'm not sure what a gunfight has to with the Bible. Nor am I sure I want to put my life on the line for the sake of your biblical musings."

Harold pointed his gun at Chambers and sneered. "Your choice. Shoot it out or take a bullet."

The big man stared down Harold for half a minute.

"What's it gonna be, ya big lug? I don't have all day!"

As he pulled his pistol from his harness and looked sadly at Dexter, Chambers said, "We'll talk later about whether it's wise to point a gun at me ever again." Dexter swallowed and reluctantly pulled his gun.

"Well, alright then, let's get to it. Bob you walk five paces that way, and Dexter, you walk five paces the other way," Harold said, directing with his gun.

"I'd pay money for something like this, but I'm gonna get it for free," Harold mocked.

Pieces of broken glass crunched under foot as they silently paced off, stopping when they reached five.

"Okay, don't turn around until after I've counted to ten. Got it?!"

Both men nodded. Harold slowly counted to ten. Bob Chambers took a deep breath, thinking he'd rather be anywhere but here. He liked Dexter, as he did Mason. Dexter was the closest thing he had to a son. In less crazy circumstances, he might have served as a father to a lad like Dexter, but that was not the situation they were in. As Harold's counting got closer to ten, the big lug's mind cleared, thinking only about quickly pulling the trigger. Knowing he was much faster and more experienced than the boy, he visualized victory.

"Nine… Ten! Draw, you heels!"

Bob Chambers pulled his gun and whipped around. But as he did, he felt a sharp pain pierce his chest. Looking straight ahead, he saw Dexter's smoking gun pointed at him. He faltered as he felt the life being gently pulled out of his body. It had never occurred to him that the kid might be faster... Drifting off into the death, he understood that is the way the ball bounces. It was time to go and answer for all his transgressions. With that final thought, he fell to the ground.

Rory cackled with glee at the sight of Bob falling to the earth like a piece of pig iron.

"Not how I saw all of this playing out, but hey, life's full of surprises!" Harold said as he re-holstered his gun. "Okay, before we saddle up, anyone want to say a few words for the dead?"

"Yeah, I'd like to say that some people are luckier than others!" Rory said with his hand over his heart.

"What about you, Dexter?"

Dexter nodded as he looked down sadly at the dead man.

"Ahh! Man up! You think he liked you? That heel was in it only for himself and would've shot you deader than a doornail. So come on, let's go!" Rory said.

The remaining three hoods piled into the sedan. The car's motor revved to life and the vehicle sped out of town, kicking up rocks and a brown plume of dust.

As they headed out of town, a leathery-faced old prospector poked his head through the glassless window of the old saloon. He then walked out onto the street and looked down at the dead hood's corpse.

"The automobile was headed thataway," the prospector said as he pointed west. Dan Fowler briefly looked in the direction the of the old timer's hand. This simple observation supported Fowler's hunch about their destination, Vegas. Even though this bunch was predictable, the dead body of one of their own showed that they would be ruthless and desperate when it came time for a face off.

Another G-Man wiped sweat from his brow before it turned to salt. He took a drink from a canteen and tucked his tie in his jacket to keep it from flapping around in the hot desert wind. He busied himself going through the dead man's pockets, rummaging for a clue. He pulled his hand from an inside pocket, holding a scrap of paper.

"What do you have, Scruggsy?" Vane asked.

"It's an address in Utah!"

With knowing grins, Dan Fowler and Kendall looked at each other.

Dexter dipped his hand in the clear, green water of the river and took a big drink. As icy liquid ran down his throat, his whole body shivered. *How could it be so hot, and the water so damn cold*, he thought. But the water must've had magical powers; exhilaration washed over him. As he faced the heavens, the sky seemed a lot bluer, the hills a lot browner. As he thought about the past, what was once blurry came more into focus. He had seen a lot of killing in the last few days. Why, just yesterday, he came within inches of his own demise.

Dexter's train of thought was interrupted, when he heard the voices of two new dames that the brothers had picked up. They were Bob Chambers' nieces.

The brothers had played upon their sympathies and convinced the girls that their uncle would want only the best for them. Who could provide that any better than Harold and Rory Murdock?

The more he thought about the brothers and the girls, a sour feeling pervaded the young man's stomach. But pragmatism creeped back into his conscience like a slithering snake. He was stuck in the life he chose, and there was nothing he could do about the girls' well-being. The best he could do was try not to get killed, and when the time came, get as far away from the brothers as possible—and maybe take the girls with him.

As he was floating in the river, enjoying the solitude, Dexter noticed a buzzard circling overhead. He concentrated on the flight of the bird to try to drown out the noisy foursome.

"This fire is hot!" Mabel said as she gazed at the ferocious yellow and orange flames that reached for the sky. The sight of the fire thrilled her— there was a sense of power in the blaze not unlike that of the two brothers. She had always wondered why her Uncle Bob had never been around as she and Audrey were growing up. Now she knew why. If only she had known what he had been up to, she could have linked up with these men sooner. Like every other small-town girl, she wanted out. Even though she shuddered a little when Rory looked at her, she admired the countenance of the two criminals. Audrey hadn't wanted to go along, but Mabel convinced her that these two men could get them away from their wicked parents.

"Things are going to get much hotter before we're through!" Harold said, making sparks when he threw another log on the fire.

"Where we going?" Audrey asked.

Dexter looked at the girl as he lit a cigarette. "St. George."

"What's in St. George?" Audrey asked.

"Your uncle told us there's a big…?" Dexter's words were cut short by Harold who mimed a slit to the throat.

"We got things to do. People to see. Then it's off to Paris with you two!" Harold said.

"Yeah, Paris!' Rory chimed in.

Harold was determined to make it to Paris—and he was dead set on *doing it* with two broads in tow. People had to have goals. Paris was his. It was a place his mom had loved, and he figured if there was anything he could do for her sainted soul, it was to get him, his brother and some honest women to that city. He was pretty sure that Rory shared his desire; but if he didn't, so be it.

"Either you girls been to Paris?"

Both girls shook their head.

"Paris is just peachy. You'll love it there," Rory added.

Sally Vane wore just enough makeup to accentuate her finest features. She was a tough broad, and the rest of the team knew it. But every so often she had to take a brief look in the mirror to remind herself that she was a woman. Grabbing a handkerchief, she dabbed her eyes, wiping away some stray mascara. A brush through her hair completed the look. But right now, her life depended on staying frosty. She loved field work, and she loved Dan Fowler and all the other agents. But it was a *brotherly* love. (To have a meaningful relationship, she would have to be far away from the bureau.) She packed up her gear, stuffed her compact in her jacket pocket, and walked out of the bathroom.

As Vane entered the main room of the makeshift field office, she looked upon empty chairs and card tables. The rest of the agents had gone to lunch. The view out the window was the same sight she saw every place they stopped: blue skies, trees and sunshine, as well as a nondescript Main Street. *It was so nice out there*, she thought, *that if one didn't know any better, they would think the world was a great place.* "But it was", Sally said to herself. That's why she sacrificed marriage and family—to make sure that it stayed that way.

The team was now in Snyder, Texas, camped out in the back of the post office. They needed access to the telegraph. The noise of the ticking machine brought Sally Vane back into the ball game. She calmly walked over and pulled the paper out of the machine. As she read the message, her face brightened.

"They didn't tell you where they were going?" Kendall asked. The craggy-faced man, who wore a rumpled gray suit jacket over faded coveralls, shook his head that was snow-capped with gray-white fringe. His wife, dressed in a frumpy floral jumper that covered a plump frame, shook hers in unison.

The wire that Vane picked off the telegraph was a report about two missing girls in Provo, Utah. As luck would have it, they were related to the dead hood that they discovered back at the ghost town.

Now in Provo, Utah, the agents were sitting in the parlor of Mr. and Mrs. Price, a very plain looking middle-aged farm couple. Two straight-backed chairs, a frayed velvet davenport, and two hutches comprised the modest room. In front of each agent rested a cup of hot tea and a pewter dish with two hard biscuits.

Sally Vane took a polite bite of one of the biscuits and thought maybe she had chipped a tooth. After moving her tongue around in her mouth to make sure that was not so, she cleared her throat. This prompted the two agents to politely take a bite of their biscuits as well.

"Did either of the two men or their associates ever contact you?" Fowler asked.

"We never saw them before in our lives," Mr. Price replied.

Dan Fowler looked at the man, who was wiping perspiration from his forehead. It was obvious to the G-Man that Mr. Price was lying. One did not have to be an expert to see the tells. The fidgeting, the clamminess and the darting eyes spoke volumes about the man's integrity.

Since the man's brother was mixed up with them, it was obvious why they might want to protect the two robbers. But the fact that their daughters were missing was a different story. Wouldn't he want to give the agent some insight as to where they might have gone?

"Mr. Price, I do not want to be rude or impertinent, but we got a wire reporting that your daughters are missing. We care more about getting your daughters back then anything else," Vane said. It wasn't a complete lie; Sally Vane and the others did care about getting the daughters back safely. But, in all reality, both she and the others knew that apprehending the robbers was their main priority. The problem was that their assumed advantage was evaporating. For whatever reason, the Prices didn't seem too concerned about the disappearance of their children.

"Just out of curiosity, if you aren't worried about your daughters, why did you report them missing?"

"We *didn't* report them. We don't know who did. We figure they'll come back when they're good and ready."

Sally Vane did her best to tamp down her frustration. She looked over at Dan Fowler, who remained stoic.

Fowler was resigned to the fact that the parents were not going to be much help. He had moved on in thought. Since the couple was not going to divulge any information, he needed to find other ways to learn the whereabouts of the girls.

Fowler catalogued what he knew thus far about the family. First, they were relatives of Bob Chambers, the now-deceased bank robber. Second, they had two daughters who had allegedly run off with the Murdock Brothers. With the meager living conditions of the parents in mind, he concluded that either they weren't reaping the benefits of their relative's ill-gotten gains or, they were hiding the largesse. As he decided to go with his initial thought, he noticed that one of the end tables was cluttered.

"Then who made the report?" Kendall asked.

Mrs. Price shrugged. "Maybe their schoolteacher."

Kendall intuitively glanced at Dan Fowler, who subtly signaled Vane to keep the Prices distracted.

"So, who would this schoolteacher be?" Sally Vane probed.

"Deats, Miss Deats, a real busy body."

As they were talking, Fowler moved slowly toward the end table and started casually thumbing through the letters and papers, looking for the smallest detail. He knew he would find something, but he had to be quick! If the couple caught on to what he was doing, they would kick the agents out immediately. Sure enough, he found what he was looking for—a bank statement from Farmers and Ranchers Trust in St. George. That was where the robbers and the daughters would be.

"Come on, let's go!" Fowler said.

The others in the room, even Fowler's associates, were taken aback at his abruptness as he quickly grabbed his coat and hat.

"But don't you want to finish your tea?" Mrs. Price asked with puzzlement.

"I think we're done here!" Fowler replied, motioning to the others to hurry it along.

The couple stood on their porch and stared at them as they drove away. They reminded Fowler of the painting of a farming couple that he once saw in a newspaper. He did his best to bury his contempt for them, but it was hard. Were they afraid? Or did they just not care about their children? That question was just going to have to hang. Right now, he was off to St. George, Utah. He prayed he was not too late.

"What'd you find in there, Dan?" Kendall asked from the backseat of the car.

"A bank statement from the Ranchers and Farmers Trust in St. George. I'll wager that the gang is going to hold it up! We need to get there fast before more lives are lost. Most likely the Prices will get word to them that we are coming and to be prepared for action!"

As they walked into Maggie's Diner, the aroma of eggs, bacon and hash browns washed over Sally Vane, Dan Fowler and Kendall. Fowler surveyed the joint, and if he wasn't a man on a mission, this would be his kind of place. The doilies, the landscape paintings and the tins hanging on the

What did you find in there?"

walls made the place homey. It was much different than those futuristic city diners with gleaming chrome that were too cold and impersonal. The thought left him as quickly as it came. Dan Fowler could only think about what he needed to do to get this job done.

It wasn't long before the group saw Harold get up and go to the counter.

"Hey, toots!" Harold yelled to a tarty waitress who had her back to him. When she turned, Harold beheld a wilted flower whose weary eyes had not only seen the customers in her diner come and go, but other things as well. As wizened and tired as she was, Harold's imposing presence caused her to straighten up as if a plank of wood had suddenly braced her back.

"Yes, sir!"

"More coffee and get me some of the sponge cake with the sweet frosting."

The woman hastily pulled a new cup from the shelf and filled it with some fresh hot coffee.

"Ah, ah, ah!" Harold scolded. "Come on, I don't work in a food joint, but I do know that you got to ask the customer if he'd like cream and sugar."

The waitress swallowed hard and looked at Harold. "I'm sorry sir. Do you want cream and sugar?"

"Yeah, sure, why not?" Harold replied.

She did what he asked.

"Oh, and don't forget the cake!"

Dan Fowler and the team watched Harold as he scolded the waitress. Harold must have sensed a presence, because he turned and stared right at the head agent. Fowler motioned to his other team members to give him some space, and then sauntered over to the hoodlum.

"Let's you and I chat somewhere private!" Fowler said leaning into Harold and firmly grabbing his lapel.

"Certainly," Harold replied, smiling at the agent.

The two calmly walked over to an unoccupied booth and sat down. Fowler waved off the waitress who had tried to serve him coffee.

"Goddamn men," she muttered as she tramped away.

Harold glanced quickly at her and smirked. "Broads, sometimes they need a good a smack!"

Dan Fowler didn't respond. With his hands folded into a steeple, he calmly stared down Harold. Harold stared back. He wasn't used to this. In most cases he was the one who was doing the intimidating. Finally, Harold's eyes dropped down to the tabletop.

"Look, I know who you are, you're famous," Harold said.

"*Your* reputation precedes you as well," Fowler replied.

"So, whatever you want to say, Copper, say it quick, because I got things to do, you know?"

"It's those things you have to do that concern me," Fowler replied. "Especially those things that have to do with Farmers and Ranchers Trust."

"Oh, that thing," Harold said with a smirk.

"Since your time is limited, I'll be brief. Give it up, Murdock!" Fowler said grabbing the other man's arm.

"And why should I do that?" Harold asked, clenching his fists.

"Because, we got you outnumbered, and will cut you and your gang down the minute you walk into the bank!"

Harold chuckled. "Well, you see, you got one small problem."

"What's that?"

"Play poker much?"

"Get to your point, Murdock!"

The gangster sighed and reached into his pocket. Fowler quickly grabbed the man's hand. Harold quickly reacted. "Easy, lawman, I'm just going for my torch and smokes."

"I think you'll have to forgo the cigarette," Fowler menaced.

"All right, have it your way, Copper!" Harold snapped. When his hand was back on the counter, he said, "Now, how 'bout you take your hands off *me*—unless you're going to arrest me."

"Like I said, give it up, Murdock!"

"Well, you see, getting back to poker, your problem is, you're holding a lousy hand, and you aren't that good at bluffing."

Cocking his head and arching his eyebrows, Fowler said, "I'd think someone like you would know that I hedge my bets."

"If you lay one pinky on me, my brother and our associate, will kill the two broads and start shooting everybody in this grease joint!"

Fowler rotated in his seat and saw what he expected to see, Rory standing there grinning. The hood pulled back his jacket revealing a pistol tucked in the belt of his pants. Dan Fowler had known he wouldn't be able to nab the gang in the diner. The meeting had gone like he thought it would. He had just wanted to see what they would be up against.

"Well, there is one thing that I don't do Mr. Murdock and that is play games of chance. I prefer chess. In chess, you must think at least three moves ahead of your opponent, and with you, that isn't very hard to do. Enjoy the rest of your meal, one of your last that won't be served on a metal tray," Fowler said as he got up.

Harold sneered at the agent. "I mean it, Copper, you try anything, we'll torch this town, everyone will be…" Harold mimed slitting his throat.

Fowler smiled at the gangster and walked out.

"No bait money either or I'll blow your pretty brains all over the walls of this bank!" Rory shouted at the teller, who nervously put stacks of banded hundreds into the gunny sack, expecting the hood to fill her with lead at any moment. She shook so much that she dropped one of the packs of money.

"Ah, ah, ah! Leave it on the floor, missy!" Harold commanded. "We know all the tricks!"

As the two Murdocks focused on the teller, Dexter held the rest of the employees who were lying face down on the floor, at bay with a shotgun.

Out of the corner of his eye he saw the security guard inching toward him. He looked quickly at the brothers whose backs were to him. Then he walked over and put his foot on the security guard.

"Stay down or you'll get shot!" Dexter quietly cautioned.

"Hey, what's going on over there? I said no talking!" Harold shouted.

"Uh, the old man says he's sick!" Dexter replied, thinking quickly.

"Tough nuggies! Tell him to keep it all in until we go," Harold commanded.

Harold and Rory filled up their sacks with the cash from the teller's drawers.

"Alright, let's cheese it," Harold said, satisfied that the bags were full.

"What about the vault?" Rory asked.

For a few seconds, Harold pondered the iron door of the vault. "Nope, too risky with G- Men breathing down our necks. We gotta go before our luck runs out!"

Rory shrugged, checked out everyone in the bank, and pulled out his pistol.

"None of that!" said Harold, "Don't wanna draw any attention to ourselves!"

Rory shrugged and looked down at the security guard, cackling as he gave the man a swift kick in the stomach. The man groaned.

"Puke your guts out, for all I care!" Rory shouted as he and the other two exited the bank.

Dexter slid in on the driver's side of the Lincoln as Rory and Harold jumped in the back, with the girls sandwiched in between them. He gunned the motor and hightailed it out of town. Very discreetly, Fowler, Vane and Kendall followed them. Three other cars took up the silent pursuit as well.

Bullion was becoming a boomtown. Full of honky tonks and gambling houses. There was so much traffic that the agents eventually lost sight of the gang. But they knew the Murdock Brothers would turn up. At some point, they had to blow off steam. Fowler and the team starting asking around the clubs knowing that most likely the brothers would be creating a disturbance, giving the bartenders and dealers incentive to be cooperative.

The wheels spun on the slot machines as gamblers, mostly women, pulled down on the arm. Occasionally a bell would ring, followed by coins clattering into the metal tray below the machine. While the women played the slots, the men, either boyfriends or husbands, would play the table games.

Both Rory and Harold were shooting craps. (Since the broads were still shaken up by the robbery, they had decided to leave them behind.) By the look on Rory's face they were losing big. Harold fumed as Rory threw the dice. "I've never seen anyone with colder hands than you, brother. It's like they're ice cubes!" Rory glowered at his brother. Then he closed his eyes, put the dice to his mouth and blew on them.

"Sure, you wanna blow on those dice, fella? They seem to be cool enough!" said a balding heavy-set man in a porkpie hat. This brought howls of laughter from the crowd. Rory's eyes filled with murderous rage. Harold sensed what his brother was about to do and snapped his fingers to get Rory's attention.

"Just throw the dice!" Harold ordered.

Rory gave them a good toss and watched them roll and bounce off the other side of the table. His eyes lit up when he saw the results. He let out a war whoop. "Shoot it all," he said.

Before Harold could protest, Rory threw the dice again. This time his face deflated like a balloon.

"Drats!" he said. "You rigged the dice!"

"Sir?" asked the portly croupier with the green eyeshade.

"You rigged the dice!" Rory shouted again.

Harold noticed the croupier motion to a man in a suit, who turned his head signaling to another man in a suit. Then all of the sudden two other men appeared. All bore stony expressions on their faces. After some quick mental calculations, Harold shouted at his brother.

"Let's find Dexter and go! The next joint should be hotter!"

Two clubs later, the trio staggered out of another lounge. Since they hadn't had any luck gambling, they thought they'd try drinking, and drink they did! Rory and Harold cleaned out every bar on the main drag and drank two off-duty cigarette girls under the table. After they got rough with the dames, who refused to go back to the hotel with them, they got tossed out of the place. Dexter did his best to keep up with the brothers' shenanigans. All in all, it was a good night.

It was the dead silence of the street that quickly sobered up Harold. It was as if he had stepped through a door to another dimension. Even the noise from inside the gaming house had died down. The others noticed it, too. Harold motioned to stay quiet and began scanning their immediate environment.

A crumpled piece of paper rolled swiftly across a windless street. A creaking sound from a door with rusty hinges made Rory jittery. It was the man in a raincoat sitting on street bench that made Harold drew his gat.

"Time to go boys, they found us," Harold whispered.

"What?" Rory replied.

"That man is reading a newspaper upside down, that's what!"

"Coppers?" Dexter asked.

"Yeah, Coppers, genius. Now let's move it!"

"Not so fast, Murdocks!"

Harold turned and saw Fowler, with his gun drawn, staring at him. The trio then noticed a gun barrel poking through the newspaper that the other agent had been reading.

"Just two of you?" Rory asked.

Dan Fowler let out a hearty laugh. "I know you're not that stupid! Give up now and no one has to get hurt."

Dexter couldn't see any other agents, but a damp, cold wave of panic had washed over him. Up until now he'd been numb. But now memories of his childhood came into focus, which soon faded into a future he now realized he would never have. Disappointment gave way to fright, then rage.

"Die, Pig!" Dexter shouted as he drew down lightning fast on Fowler.

But the boy was no match for the G-Man's reflexes. Fowler fired faster. Sick gray smoke billowed from his gun as the bullet plugged the boy right between the eyes.

"It's on, brother!" Rory yelled as he drew his gun and fired a couple of wild shots.

This caused a hailstorm of bullets to come their way riddling the sidewalk, the buildings and everything in between.

"Looks like we're outnumbered again!" Harold shouted, as he ran, shooting behind him, for the cover of the car.

"And that's the way we like it!" Rory yelled as he sighted and dropped a nondescript agent from the roof top.

Harold was pretty sure that the cops would get them if they were out on the street like this. Bullets popped all around his feet, causing him to bolt like a jack rabbit to the cover of another car.

He peered out from behind the car. He could see dark figures coming out of the woodwork; all of them well heeled. The scene reminded him of a nightmare that he had as a child; he was at his bedroom window and saw men in black flowing robes coming at him on big black stallions. Knives were in their teeth. Since that time, it was as if Harold had been running from them, leaving death and destruction in his wake.

Under the glow of the pale moonlight he saw what he needed to see. The new town was built to hide the old one. The rickety buildings and store fronts were not just the ghosts of what this gambling oasis once was. It served as a reminder that all the glitz could not mask the fact that nothing had changed. This was still the Old West and the outlaws still roamed the country, even if they were driving cars instead of riding horses. Harold saw the significance, and he felt the romance, too.

"Rory, over there!" Harold said as he pointed to the buildings.

Dan Fowler felt the tension in his muscles. He and the others were at a disadvantage—the brothers had a head start on them when they made a run for the old buildings. Now he felt as though he was the one being watched and hunted—and he didn't like it. But he had no choice. It was now or never.

Either these brothers had to surrender, or they had to die. Dan Fowler preferred to take them alive, but at this point he'd settle for dead. As a bullet popped at his feet, it was becoming clear that "dead" might be how this was going to end.

He and the others stood in a wedge formation in the middle of the street. They were far from the lights of the town, relying on the natural illumination which made the buildings look like silhouettes. Every small sound put the agents on a more heightened state of alert.

"Go find cover. I'll draw their fire," Dan Fowler whispered as more bullets popped around them.

Two agents ran for the old livery stable. Sally Vane and Kendall ran to the batwing doors of an old saloon.

Now it was just Fowler standing in the street of what once was a one-horse town. No images of cowboys or Indians popped into his mind. He was fully focused on the darkness, and the buildings were obstacles rather than history.

"It's just me now, Murdocks!" Dan Fowler shouted.

But there was silence. Fowler sidestepped as two bullets whizzed by his feet. "Why don't you come on out and face me like men, instead of hiding like rats!"

This elicited a volley of gunfire and Fowler ran for the cover of a beer barrel on the wooden sidewalk. As he ducked, he could feel the air from the bullets as they splintered the windowless frame of the storefront behind him. When he poked his head up, another bullet almost parted his hair down the middle.

"You're no match for us, Copper! We'll make Swiss cheese out of your miserable hide!"

This was followed by another volley of gunfire. As he waited for the bullets to stop, Fowler pressed hard against the barrel. He could wait them out. Surely, they would run out of ammo. But since they had him pinned, they could easily steal off into the night and live to create more mayhem and destruction. So, come hell or high water, he had to lure the brothers out into the street.

"You know, I'm pretty sure I could best both of you in a gun fight Old West style! What do you boys think about that?" Dan waited for their response which seemed like an eternity. But his patience paid off.

"What, we come out into the open, and you Coppers cut us down!"

"You think we'd do that?" Fowler shouted back.

"Why not? It's what we'd do!" Harold yelled.

A smile crept across Fowler's face. With Harold's response came an opening—a chink in the hood's armor—a weakness that the agent intended to exploit.

"You see, that's where we differ, I'm a G-Man, a man of honor. I live by a code of conduct that is one of high integrity!"

More shots rang out, causing Fowler to duck.

"All cops are thieving bastards and liars. You're no different!" Harold shouted back.

"G-Men are different. Besides, I'm confident in a faceoff. With just two bullets, I could drop both you and your worthless brother," Fowler replied. He waited for what seemed a long period of time. Then his finely trained ears heard two sets of footsteps making their way to the center of Main Street.

"Come on out G-Man and face the music!" Rory cackled.

"Yeah, let's see what you're made of!" Harold shouted.

With his gun trained on the two brothers, Dan Fowler slowly got up.

"We face off just like the Old West!" Dan Fowler shouted. He moved toward the two dark figures.

"I'll count to three!" Harold yelled.

"Nope! *I'll* count to three! You two would probably shoot me in the back."

"What, you don't think we have a code?" Rory taunted.

"I do, and it's to shoot people like me in the back!" Fowler replied.

Both brothers laughed.

"He's got a point!" Harold said. "Okay, let's get on with it!"

Dan Fowler counted... and at the end of "three", heavy gun fire came from all directions. Fowler watched as the bullets violently shook the life out of both brothers, as they finally dropped to the ground. Fowler could not help but be strangely impressed by their silence. It was quite common for tough men to bawl like babies when their end finally came. But not these men.

"A tough assignment, but that's why you got it!" the Director said.

Fowler cracked a smile as he heard the man deliver the same line he always did whenever an agent finished a job.

"I couldn't have done it without the rest of my great team," Dan Fowler replied.

The Director nodded as he shuffled some papers and handed Fowler a thick folder.

"Well, there is no time for you to rest on your laurels. I am sending you to New York. The Phantom Detective needs your help. All the details are in the file," the Director said.

"Hmm!" Dan Fowler mused as he thumbed through the papers. "Nothing worse than a shady politician!"

"We are more interested in who's *funding* that politician. We suspect it's Nicholas Spano, the sinister financier!"

"Sinister, indeed. I'll find out if he's up to no good!"

THE END

Gangster Westerns & Other Thoughts About Dan Fowler

I have always loved the idea of the continuation of the Wild West, well into the 1930s, and that it grew wilder, and much more violent. Automobiles replaced the horse. Spats and suits replaced boots and britches. The cowboy hat gave way to the fedora. Finally, I love how the Six Gun turned into the "Tommy Gun".

However, what didn't change was the mayhem and carnage which both sides caused when they squared off, or the tumbleweed ridden towns that they both terrorized. Consequently, the true exploits of these early to mid-twentieth century bandits and lawmen created a sub-genre called the Gangster Western. I wanted Dan Fowler to be thrust into that environment. This notion of the Gangster Western is what birthed "The Bloody Murdocks".

Traditionally, pulp stories tend to be overwritten with a lot of purple prose. For the purposes of this story, I toned that down and sprinkled in some western rawhide. But with that said, I did not want the environment too muddy or dusty so touches of "Batman 66" were added. For example, the lush hideaway of Buster Pardue and his gang; and Rory and Harold Murdock's crazy antics, which owe a debt to the likes of the Joker.

While trying to stay true to the spirit of the Golden Era pulp, I also needed to satisfy the modern reader's appetite for cinematic action and lots of it. As a result, the action and violence tended to be a lot more horrific and gratuitous than one would have experienced in a Dan Fowler tale of yore. Instances of these would include Rory setting the deputy on fire, the gunfight in the ghost town, and the final scene. Back in the day, Dan Fowler might have been more honorable, but I wanted to give the reader the idea that G-Men were not as pure as the legends would have you believe. In this story, there are a few instances where Dan Fowler went a little outside of protocol, such as his interrogation of Buster Pardue in the holding cell, as well as the final stand off with the Murdocks where Dan Fowler has the G-Men flat-out execute the brothers by riddling them with bullets, after he got the Murdocks to believe he was going to engage them in a gunfight. If there was ever a code in the Old West, it no longer existed in the twentieth century.

Dan Fowler is a fascinating character in pulp. While he is not a superhero, he is extraordinarily capable, and in some cases, measures up to the finest of caped crusaders. Since Fowler doesn't wear a mask, he doesn't have to be unassuming and downplay his abilities compared to the masked and caped variety of pulp heroes. As a result, he can be more upfront about who he is, enabling him to be more of an alpha male. This gave me the opportunity to present him as a slightly more hard-boiled character similar to Philip Marlowe or Mike Hammer. With this approach to the character and because pulp is my favorite genre of writing, I will no doubt revisit Dan Fowler.

WHIT HOWLAND—is an accomplished author. Along with Airship 27, he has written stories for Pro Se Press and Untreed Reads; all in the pulp fiction and mystery genres. He currently resides in Illinois with his wife and three cats. When he is not busy writing, his time spent as a Campus Security officer at a small liberal arts college gives him fodder for new story ideas.

Dead Man Shooting
by Gene Moyers

The gray stone walls of Clarksville Federal Penitentiary looked grim and depressing even in the bright sunshine of an August day. The large barred gate, wide enough to accept a prison bus, and the small steel door inset into the wall near it did nothing to relieve the depressing atmosphere surrounding the high walls. Nor did the ornate cornices and skilled stonework of the attached administration building serve to brighten its appearance. The barred windows ruined any pleasing aesthetics.

Across the parking lot from the barred gate Dan Fowler and Larry Kendal sat in their government sedan. Both men were tall, well-built young men cut from that exceptional cloth that seemed all agents of the FBI seemed to be cut from. Kendal, the younger of the two men, took off his hat and scratched his curly, dark hair, "Why do you think they're turning Duke Carsten loose, Dan?"

Sitting next to his partner, Dan Fowler, ace operative of the Federal service, replied thoughtfully, "I don't know. He's less than two years into a ten year stretch. He shouldn't even be up for parole for another three years. That's why we're here. I want to talk to him. I also want to talk to the warden and find out what's going on."

Carsten was a convicted bank robber. Two years before he had been wounded during a robbery. His gang had fled leaving him to face justice alone. Two people had been shot during the hold up and the judge had sentenced Carsten to ten years in prison after the jury had found him guilty.

As Dan thought about Carsten's history a siren sounded briefly from inside the prison. Larry stiffened and instinctively reached for the pistol under his arm. Dan laughed and placed a gentle hand on his arm, "Relax, Larry. It's just the noon siren."

Larry laughed and shook his head, "Sorry, I guess I get a little nervous around a lot of cons…even when they're behind bars."

As Dan was about to reply he stiffened, "And there's our con now. Pull over there." Dan pointed to the small steel door next to the main gate. A guard was opening it and a man in a suit carrying a small valise stepped out. The guard looked like he wanted to shake hands with the man but seemed to think better of it. Instead they exchanged a few words and the guard reentered the prison yard and closed the door.

Meanwhile Larry had started the car and driven across the lot to pull up five yards in front of the released convict. Dan got out, placed his hat on his head of dark hair and walked up to the man. George "Duke" Carsten was a stocky, brown haired man a three inches short of Dan's six foot two height. He had a scar on the right side of his chin. As Dan approached he stood motionless, his face unmoving.

Dan stopped six feet away and stared the ex-con in the eye, "Hello Duke."

His expression unchanging Carsten replied in a dead voice, "Fowler."

Dan nodded, "Yeah, I head you were getting out. Thought I'd drop by and wish you well."

Carsten grimaced, "Come off it G-Man. Say what you gotta say and get lost. I got things to do. I'm not on the government's time anymore."

"Okay, here it is. I don't know why the parole board saw fit to let you out but I want to tell you that the Bureau is watching you. In fact I'm going to make a special point keeping an eye on what you're up to. If you were smart you'd take this chance and clean up your life. Oh, I forgot if you had any smarts you'd have a real job, wouldn't you."

Surprisingly Carsten didn't rise to this insult as Dan had hoped. Instead he stood mute, just staring through Dan without expression. Dan had hoped getting the hood angry might make him say something interesting. Instead he looked uncaring and said, "You through?" A pause then, "Good I got things to do." He waved at something behind Dan and brushed past him.

Dan turned and watched Carsten walk around the rear of the government car and toward a sedan that had entered the lot and had pulled up fifty feet away. Without a word to the driver Carsten tossed his valise in the back seat and got into the passenger side of the car. Before he slammed the door Dan got a glimpse of a leg and a wide floppy hat. The driver was a woman. Without another glance the car accelerated hard throwing dust from its rear wheels and disappeared out of the lot.

Shaking his head Dan walked to the car where Larry leaned out the driver's side window, "So...what'd he say?"

Looking thoughtful Dan remarked, "Nothing. He said nothing. No anger, no resentment, he didn't even looked pleased. Hmmnn . . ." He waved an arm, "Park over there Larry. I'm going to have a word with the warden."

As Larry parked the car Dan walked to the administration building. Showing his badge to the armed guard he was quickly directed to the warden's office. Five minutes later he was shaking hands with Warden Moffett. Moffett was a thin, gray haired man who wore steel spectacles. He had the no-nonsense look of a man who could handle the tough job of policing a Federal prison. Once seated Dan asked, "Warden, I'm interested in George Carsten. Isn't it unusual for a man like Carsten to be released early?"

Moffett clasped his hands on his desk and nodded, "You are absolutely right agent Fowler. No one was more surprised than I when I received notice from the parole board the Carsten was to be paroled. I was so surprised that I had my secretary call the board for confirmation."

Dan leaned forward, "Then you were worried that someone was attempting a phony release order?"

The warden nodded, "Or perhaps it was a clerical error. I even briefly considered bribery but quickly discarded that idea. The parole board is beyond reproach. I am personally acquainted with every member of the board and they are all honest men."

Dan mulled that over for a moment, "Carsten wasn't even up for parole for another three years. How could the board do such a thing?"

Moffett shook his head, "As far as I know the board has never set eyes on Carsten. The release simply sighted compassionate reasons.'"

"Compassionate reasons, what does that mean?"

"I couldn't say but perhaps you should speak to the prison chaplain and the prison doctor."

Dan frowned, "Why? What would they know?"

The warden shrugged, "I don't know but each of them received a copy of the release form. And that is somewhat irregular."

Dan stood up, hat in hand, "Well, if that's all you can tell me warden then I thank you."

Moffett offered his hand, "I'm sorry I couldn't tell you anything more Agent Fowler."

Outside the office Larry Kendal was waiting. The two agents walked back to their car Larry asking, "Well, what did you find out?"

Dan replied, "Nothing. The warden says Carsten was released for 'compassionate reasons."

"What does that mean?"

They reached the car and Dan shrugged as he opened his door, "I don't know. Maybe I'll make a few calls when we get back to the office and try to find out what's going on." Larry nodded and got behind the wheel. Soon they were on their way back to Chicago.

Two days later a gleaming Packard sedan pulled to a stop in front of an Italian restaurant in South Bend Indiana. Three people got out. The first man out was a big man who held up a hand to the other passengers while he looked carefully around. Seeing nothing suspicious he held the car door open wide as a well-dressed man and woman exited. The three entered the restaurant where they appeared to be well known. They were shown to a nice table and seated. The big man was seated at the next table over in a position where he could watch the restaurant easily. A waiter appeared and they ordered. The restaurant was reasonably filled and the buzz of conversation filled the room.

Minutes passed and orders were brought to the three newcomers. The well-dressed couple conversed casually. Their obvious bodyguard sat quietly. He ate slowly and paused often to look over the restaurant carefully. He looked up as a couple entered. The woman on the man's arm was young and attractive. She laughed at something her companion said as the head waiter led them toward a table. Her stocky companion's face could not be seen as he was removing his hat at that moment. The large man relaxed and looked down to scoop up a forkful of ravioli.

At that moment a woman screamed. There was a frozen moment as the two people at the table looked up in shocked surprise then everything happened at once. Duke Carsten was striding forward a large automatic in his hand. The well-dressed man held up his hands, one still holding his fork, and screamed, "No Duke!" just before Carsten fired. The first bullet hit him the chest and as he went over backwards in his chair the second bullet caught him in the throat. Blood flew everywhere. At the same time the large body guard shoved back from his table and was pulling a gun from under his coat. As the gun cleared leather and came up Carsten's young companion stepped to one side and opened up with a hammerless pistol she had pulled from her purse. All three .32 slugs caught the big man in the chest. Hammered backwards his automatic discharged once shattering a bottle of Chianti on the next table. He slammed into the wall and slid down it to the floor.

The girl turned and ran for the front door stowing her pistol in her purse as she went. Carsten backed after her, his .45 flicking left and right as he covered their retreat. As they exited the restaurant the shocked silence broke. People began yelling and a woman's screaming was added to the hysteric sobbing of the woman at the table of death.

In the Chicago office of the FBI, located in the Federal building, Dan sorted through stacks of papers on his desk. He sighed as he found the report he was looking for. As usual he was behind on his paperwork, probably because he let it pile up. Dan hated paperwork. He much preferred be out in the field. The thrill of the chase as he pursued America's most wanted criminals was what he lived for. He had just initialed the bottom of the report when Larry walked in holding a folder. He held it out saying, "Have you seen this?"

Dan took the folder and opened it, "What is it?"

"It seems that Charles Nash got blown up in a South bend restaurant two days ago."

"Really? We've been looking for him for quite a while."

Larry smiled wryly, "Well, it looks like someone found him first."

Dan scanned the report, "Is this right? He was shot by someone named Duke?"

"Yeah, that's what the witnesses say."

Dan finished the report and looked up at his young partner, "What about this girl the witnesses talk about?"

"No real description. I bet everyone was diving for cover about then. Everyone seems to think she was young though."

Dan leaned back in his chair and thought for a moment, "A young woman picked up Carsten at the prison." He handed the report back to Larry and told him, "Follow up on this. I'm going to call the prison again." Larry nodded, took the report and left.

When he was gone Dan flipped through his rolodex until he found the right card. He dialed the federal prison and was soon connected to the warden. After greetings the warden told him, "I can't tell you any more than I already have Agent Fowler."

"I understand, sir. The reason I called was to get the phone numbers of the prison's chaplain and doctor."

"Oh. I can certainly help you there." There was a shuffling of papers then, "Okay, I have it. The chaplain isn't on our staff. He's a local minister who volunteers here." He rattled off a phone number as Dan copied it down, "As for the doctor, he's in his office. I'll have the switchboard connect you."

Dan thanked him and waited. Soon a cultured voice answered, "Dr. Philips." Dan identified himself and asked about Carsten's parole. The doctor was reticent; finally saying, "I'm afraid medical ethics forbids me from discussing Carsten's medical condition. All I can say is that he was granted a parole for compassionate medical reasons." Dan had to be satisfied with this small bit of information. He thanked the doctor and hung up.

He next dialed the number of the prison chaplain. It did not take long to be connected to Reverend Neilson. He quickly identified himself and asked about Carsten. There was a short pause before the reverend answered, "Yes, I remember George Carsten."

"Good. I am trying to find out about his parole. Can you help me?"

"I'm sorry Agent Fowler, I'm afraid I cannot speak of anything told to me in confidence."

Frustrated Dan thought for a moment before asking, "Did you speak to Carsten personally before he was released?"

"Yes, I did attempt to bring spiritual counsel to him. But I'm afraid he didn't say much."

Dan realized that he was up against professionals who took their oaths and responsibilities seriously. He wasn't going to get anywhere here. "Thank you, Reverend. I guess you can't help me."

There was a pause before the reverend spoke. "Perhaps there is a man you might be able to learn something from."

Dan perked up, "Really. What's his name?"

"Dr. Elliot Spencer. He has a practice in Chicago. I don't have the address but I'm sure he's in the phone directory."

Another doctor? Dan was skeptical, "Are you sure he'll speak to me?"

"I am sure that you should go and speak to him at his office. I believe you will understand if you do." With this cryptic remark the Reverend bid Dan good luck and said goodbye. Dan thought for a moment and reached for the thick Chicago phone book.

Two hours later Dan entered a posh doctor's office in a high rise building on Chicago's north side. He walked up to the uniformed nurse manning a counter and flashed his badge, "I'm Agent Fowler, FBI. I'd like to speak to Dr. Spencer."

Surprised the nurse replied, "Dr. Spencer is with a patient. If you'll take a seat I'm sure he will be able to see you in a few minutes." Dan reluctantly took a seat. He didn't particularly like doctor's offices or hospitals for that matter. He had seen the inside of too many of them. He fidgeted for fifteen minutes before a man came out of an inner office. Dan looked up. It was certainly not the doctor. It was a very thin, elderly man who did not appear to be in good health. He looked pale and tired. Dan waited while he spoke to the nurse and when he left Dan stood up. She held up a warning finger and disappeared.

Moments later she returned, "Doctor will see you now." She then conducted Dan to an inner office and left. The office was expensively furnished. A doctor dressed in white exam wrap stood up from behind his oak desk. Dan stepped forward hand out, "I'm Agent Dan Fowler doctor. Thank you for seeing me."

"It's my pleasure agent Fowler, what can I do for you?"

"I understand you consult with the bureau of prisons at Clarksville penitentiary."

The physician nodded carefully, "I am called in for special consultations."

Dan tried to tread carefully, "I understand that you have medical ethics to consider but I am trying to find out anything I can about the parole of George Carsten. Anything you can tell me would be helpful."

The doctor contemplated Dan carefully, "Obviously you already understand my situation. No doubt you have already spoken to the prison doctor. Otherwise you wouldn't be here. Unfortunately, I am bound by medical ethics just as he is. I can tell you nothing about Carsten's condition."

Dan had been afraid of this, "I understand, but he does have a 'condition.'

Can you at least tell me if it is serious?"

"I'm afraid I can't help you Agent Fowler."

Dan stood up wondering why Reverend Neilson had sent him here if he knew the doctor wouldn't talk to him. He smiled, "Well, thank you for your time doctor." He turned to go but a sudden thought came to him. The reverend had said Dan might learn something here. He hadn't said anyone would speak to him. As Dan opened the office door he looked back, "What did you say your specialty was doctor?"

The doctor had sat back down but looked up in surprise, "Why, I'm an oncologist, of course." Dan smiled and nodded his thanks. On his way out he spoke to the nurse, "Pardon me, but I'm not totally familiar with the medical world. Doesn't an oncologist specialize in cancer treatment?"

The nurse nodded proudly, "Yes, Dr. Spencer is a leading authority in oncology." Dan thanked her and left. As he put on his hat in the hallway he mused that the Reverend Neilson had been right. He had learned a lot.

"Gimme that bag!" Duke Carsten grabbed the leather valise from the obviously frightened man. He then gestured with his pistol, "Now, get over there behind the counter." The frightened manager scurried to do as he was told. Carsten then turned and waved his pistol in the air, "The rest of you just stay where you are! Anybody makes a move and I plug' em!"

He turned and made for the door of the bank. As he did an alarm bell began ringing loudly. Carsten swore and turned, firing toward the counter as he backed quickly toward the door of the bank. Tellers ducked behind the heavy counter. One unlucky man wasn't fast enough. He caught one of Carsten's careless slugs in the shoulder and went down with a cry of pain.

His revolver empty, Carsten pushed through the bank doors. In front of the bank, engine running was a Ford sedan. The passenger door was open wide and the young woman behind the wheel, screamed at him, "C'mon Duke! We gotta go!" Carsten dove into the car and the woman let in the clutch and they screamed down the street. "Wowww," yelled the woman, "How much did we get?"

Duke thumbed cartridges into his gun as he replied, "Can't tell yet. Step on it, baby!"

Their car was doing nearly sixty miles per hour when a police cruiser whirled into their path from a side street. It straightened up coming their way; siren screaming. Laughing uproariously the young woman steered directly at the oncoming squad car. Beside her Duke swore. She didn't hear him; she was concentrating on the shocked looks on the faces of the two policemen she could see clearly through the windshield of their car. The woman held her course. At the last second the police car swerved to the right. It jumped the side walk and hit a mailbox. Torn from its anchors, the red and blue box flew into a wooden newsstand turning it into splinters; newspapers and pulp magazines flying everywhere. The poor newsie dove over his counter just before the mailbox hit his stand and ended up in the gutter with magazines fluttering down around him.

The two shocked cops staggered out of their damaged squad car. They stared at the crumpled bumper and the steam spiraling out from under the sprung hood. By the time they turned to look, the fleeing Ford was a fast disappearing speck. Grabbing for his key one cop headed for a nearby call box to call in to headquarters. The other rubbed his bruised head and watched the two felons disappear out of town.

The next morning Dan and Larry sat down to compare notes. Larry spoke first, "It looks like Carsten and Nash went way back together. They shared a cell back in Ohio nearly ten years ago. Nash was doing a stretch for attempted murder during a shootout with a rival bootlegging gang. Duke Carsten was doing a stretch for bank robbery. The reports I read thought they might have been working together a few years ago when Duke was arrested for that busted robbery where he was shot. It wouldn't surprise me to find out that Nash was one of the gang who got a way."

Dan looked thoughtful, "So Carsten was evening the score for Nash leaving him in to take the rap." He leaned back in his chair and continued, "I know why he was released from prison."

Larry perked up, "Yeah, why?"

"I'm pretty sure he's got cancer. Nobody will say for sure, sighting medical privacy ethics but reading between the lines, I don't think Carsten's got long to live."

"Really? Why do you think that?"

"The doctor the prison doc called in specializes in cancer. He's one of the best, I guess. And if the board released Carsten for compassionate reasons it must mean he hasn't got long to live." Larry frowned, "How long do you think?"

Dan shrugged, "I don't know: months…maybe weeks, who knows? But if you only had a few months to live, what would you do?"

Larry pointed to the report of Nash's murder on the desk, "I might be real interested in settling some old scores before I checked out." Dan nodded in agreement, "We just need to find out who else he might be after."

The younger agent pointed out, "Carsten never would rat on his gang that robbed the bank when he was shot. How do we find out who they

The newsie dove over his counter...

might be?"

Dan smiled, "We start with the files. We cross check for any violent hoods that had prior contacts with both Nash and Carsten. They also must have been unaccounted for during the time when Carsten was robbing banks two years ago. When we have a short list, that's who we'll go after. I'll bet a week's pay that's where we'll find Carsten. He'll be looking for them as well.

As Larry stood up to go he asked, "You remember the woman who picked up Carsten at the prison?" Dan nodded. His partner continued, "I remembered the license number of the car and looked it up." Dan looked interested. Larry continued, "It's registered to a Doris Wagner down in Joliet. Thought I might take a trip down there and have a talk with her. Maybe she'll tell me where she took Carsten."

Dan nodded, "Good thinking. Get on that right away. Meanwhile I'll get started on these files."

The next morning Larry left for Joliet. Dan spent part of the morning in the records room. Then he began burning up the long distance wires checking facts. In the afternoon a young agent approached Dan carrying a piece of paper, "Agent Fowler? I have a report you might be interested in."

Looking up interestedly Dan nodded, "Go ahead. What is it?" From the paper the agent read, "It seems there was a bank robbery down in Terra Haute two days ago. A man identified as George Carsten assisted by an unknown female robbed a bank there of nearly twenty two thousand dollars." Dan sat up straight in his chair, "Terra Haute? Two days ago?" He stood up and walked to a map of the Midwest on the wall. He touched, South Bend on the map and then ran his finger down to Terra Haute. He paused and then ran it down to St. Louis. Turning he thanked the young agent and went back to his files.

The phone rang on Dan's desk later that day. Answering it he found Larry on the line; long distance, "Larry where are you?"

"I'm in Joliet. I just got done talking to Mrs. Wagner. It turns out that she's a middle aged widow who's never met Duke Carsten. However she did loan her car out to her grown daughter that day. The car is sitting here next to her home by the way."

"So where's the daughter?"

"It turns out that the day that after returning her mother's car young Sherry Wagner packed a bag, left and hasn't been seen since."

Dan frowned, "Young? How young?"

"Mrs. Wagner says that her daughter just turned nineteen. Apparently she's a wild one; in and out of trouble, always running with rough crowds. Her mother says she's been out of control for years. Only shows up when she needs a place to sleep."

"That's just great. Does Mrs. Wagner have any idea where she went?"

"I'm afraid not. But get this: Apparently before she was left she told her mother that this time she was going to be rich and famous."

Dan shook his head, "Good work Larry. I've got news too."

"I'm on my way back to the office now."

Dan quickly vetoed this, "No. You're on your way to St. Louis. I've put together a list of hoods that very possibly made up Carsten's last gang. Charles Nash was one of them. The other three are Frank Duvall, Tommy Ryan and Johnny Perucci. They all are known to each other and were sighted together around the time of those robberies two years ago."

Larry whistled, "So those are the guys that left Carsten holding the bag. No wonder he wants them dead. So where are they?"

"Duvall is supposedly operating out of Kansas City. Tommy Ryan is running some supposedly legitimate businesses in St. Louis. Johnny Perucci is in jail in Indianapolis. He's being tried there for attempted murder."

"So I'm going to St Louis then?"

"Right. I want you to get down there and put Ryan under surveillance. Get some help from the St. Louis office."

"Where are you going? KC?"

"No, I'm going to Indianapolis tomorrow. I figure that Perucci is pretty safe in police custody but I want to brace him about Carsten. He may give up something about Ryan and Duvall as well. When I'm done there I'll follow you to St. Louis. Let the office there know where you are and I'll get in contact."

"Right. See you in Saint Looey Dan" Larry said in a sing song voice.

Dan laughed as he hung up.

At ten the next morning Dan walked through the doors of the Federal courthouse in Indianapolis. He had driven through the night to be on hand when court started. Inquiring at the information desk he found out that Perucci's trial was in court room four on the third floor. He got in the elevator and told the operator, "Three, please." The operator nodded and started the car upward. Seconds later as they neared the third floor Dan clearly heard gunfire. The car slowed as the operator, clearly frightened, slackened his push on the lever operating the car. Dan lunged across the car and shoved the operator's hand forward, jerking his automatic from its holster at the same time. The car jerked upward and Dan pressed the open door button frantically.

The gunfire had stopped by the time the doors opened and Dan jumped out into a scene of chaos. Women were screaming; people ran to and fro. Stepping out, pistol up Dan's eyes were drawn to his left. A hand cuffed man lay in a spreading pool of blood. Nearby a police officer lay dead as well, his gun still in its holster. A second policeman lay wounded nearby. Dan bent over the man who was desperately pressing a handkerchief to a bleeding shoulder. As Dan bent to help him the man gasped out, "He went down the stairs!" He pointed shakily down the hall where Dan could see a sign sticking out into the hall above a door that read, "Stairs." Dan stood up, pointed at the wounded cop and barked a nearby man, "This man needs help!" Brushing past him he raced for the stairwell.

Dan slammed the door open with is shoulder, gun up. The landing was empty but he could hear footsteps clattering down the stairs below him. Jumping down the stairs two at a time the G-man leapt in pursuit. He used his freehand to steady himself as he jumped from step to step and across landings. In seconds he had reached the ground floor corridor. To his right a man was helping woman to her feet and cursing someone unseen. Dan sprinted past them and into the lobby. There were many people here scattered across the large open space. Dan ran for the door shouting, "Federal Agent! Clear the way!" He hurdled a security guard who had been knocked down trying to stop the assassin and raced across the lobby.

Slamming through the glass doors and onto the courthouse steps he saw a Packard sedan just accelerating away from the curb at the foot of the steps. Throwing himself down the steps to the sidewalk he brought his pistol up and sighted on the fleeing car. He squeezed off a round and saw the rear window shatter. As he brought his other hand up to steady his aim a head and shoulders appeared on the passenger side of the Packard and flame stabbed out at him.

Dan threw himself to the sidewalk on his stomach. He heard the crack of bullets flying overhead and ricocheting off the sidewalk near him. Ignoring a small bit of concrete that lanced into his cheek, Dan brought up his pistol grasped in both hands at arm's length on the concrete and began squeezing off rounds; Blam! Blam! Blam! He only stopped when the slide locked back on his now smoking automatic.

The Packard roared down the street and was now just a small, fast receding target. Dan stood up and swore under his breath. He knew he had hit the fleeing car more than once but the big Packard had absorbed the gunfire, shrugged it off and sped away. Holstering his empty weapon, Dan headed back up the steps into the courthouse.

Inside chaos reigned. Dan had to fight past panicky people fleeing through the lobby. He reached the security guard who was now standing and holding a handkerchief to a bloody head. As he paused to hear the man's story white uniformed ambulance attendants ran into the lobby and across to the elevator. They carried a stretcher. The security guard told Dan the first thing he saw was a big man running into the lobby shoving people out of the way. Before he could draw his weapon the big man had pistol whipped him to the ground and fled. He didn't have time to get a good look at him. Dan then climbed the stairs back to the third floor. There the corridor was filled with police and other court officials. He showed his badge and asked an officer how the wounded cop was. The officer replied, "Fortunately there was a doctor nearby. I think the officer is going to make it."

Dan then asked, "That was Perucci who was killed right?"

The officer nodded solemnly, "They were just bringing him up to the court room when this gunman appeared out of the crowd. He opened up without a word. Perucci got it with the first shot." He shook his head. Dan asked, "Any descriptions of the gunman?" The cop replied in the affirmative. Several bystanders had got good looks at the gunman who hadn't attempted to disguise his identity. Dan's expression hardened as he listened. All the descriptions fit Duke Carsten to a "T."

Dan gave a quick statement and description of the getaway car to the police and left. He hurried to his car. Carsten had a lead on him. It was imperative he get to the next victim before Carsten did.

Hours later the shot up Packard pulled into a filling station at a crossroads in Southern Indiana. A mechanic in the attached garage pulled his head from under the open hood of a car he was working on and walked toward the Packard wiping his hands on a rag that hung from a pocket of his overalls.

He pulled up a smile for the young girl who hopped out of the big car, "Aftenoon, Miss. Filler 'er up?"

The young girl gave him a big smile as she reached into her purse. She came up with a gleaming automatic and said, "Actually we're looking for another car. You have another car around here don't you?"

"The mechanic was slightly confused, "Uh…car?"

"Yeah," a voice grated, "A car; something that runs good. Whatta ya got?"

The mechanic turned and his mouth dropped open at the sudden appearance of a man stepping out of the rear seat of the Packard, a .45 automatic in the man's fist.

"Uh…there's Mr. Weiser's Ford over there. It's almost new, just in a for an oil change."

"Good, we'll take it. Sherry, go over to that store and see what they got."

"Okay Duke," The girl sauntered across the road toward a small market. Carsten waved his pistol at the mechanic, "Let's get that car." They moved off.

Inside, the store appeared to have a little bit of everything as many small town stores did. Sherry glanced around for a moment before the older man behind the counter asked, "Can I help you, miss?"

The girl stepped up to the counter with a smile, "Yeah, I need a bottle of whiskey and everything in the till." As she spoke she pulled her automatic out of her purse and pointed it at him, "And step on it Pops, we're in a hurry."

While the mechanic was leading Carsten around the side of the garage two *Indiana State Police* motorcycle cops cruised down the county road toward the filling station. They pulled to a halt at the four way stop sign controlling the crossroads. The older trooper, Sergeant Johnson was veteran of the older *Indiana Motor Vehicle Police Force*. His partner trooper Davies was a graduate of the new State Police academy.

The older of the two officers pointed across the intersection and said, "You know that Packard over there looks like the one we were told to be on the lookout for." His partner glanced at the car and replied, "I think you're right Frank. It's also got a hole in the rear fender that looks almighty like a bullet hole. What do ya wanna do?"

Trooper Johnson didn't hesitate, "Take the south side of the pumps. I'll take this side. Be careful. The bulletin said this guy's dangerous." The two gunned their motorcycles forward. Johnson quickly pulled up to the near side of the filling station, turned off his bike's engine, kicked down the stand and got off; his hand moving to his flap holster. The other officer motored past the pumps and turned his bike in near them and turned his bike off. As he did a car parked along the south side of the garage backed rapidly toward him.

Duke Carsten stood on the running board of the sedan, his right arm wrapped around the door post. His left held his automatic inches from the mechanic's face as he backed the car past the building toward the road. As Carsten looked over the rear of the car a motorcycle cop appeared around the gas pumps and stopped his cycle. Carsten poked his gun against the side of the mechanic's head and yelled, "Punch it!" Frightened the mechanic pressed on the accelerator pedal and the big car roared backwards.

Trooper Davies saw the car roaring toward him, the head of a man visible over the top of the car. He immediately leaped sideways off his bike. The car screeched past clipping his leg and throwing him farther away. The stunned trooper rolled over and over in the gravel. Duke leaped off the running board as the car came to a stop in a rattle of gravel. He threw a quick shot at the rolling trooper and fired again as the trooper came to a stop.

Clipped by Carsten's second shot the wounded trooper clawed at his holster. Before Carsten could finish off the wounded officer he was forced to duck as a bullet whizzed past this head. Trooper Johnson had his revolver up and was pumping slugs past the sedan at Carsten. Swearing, the gunman jerked open the door of the idling car and dragged the mechanic clear. He then dove behind the wheel.

Hearing the gunfire Sherry ran out of the corner market. Across the road from her, crouched behind his bike, Trooper Johnson was firing. Duke was firing over the car as he dragged the driver clear. Further past the station, a man on the ground was trying to bring his gun to bear. Screaming a curse Sherry ran into the road firing at the trooper behind his bike. Startled, he turned and fired once at the girl before his revolver clicked on an empty cylinder. She continued firing as she ran toward him finally finding him with her last two shots.

In the sedan Carsten backed it out onto the road in a spray of gravel. Cranking the wheel he ended up in the middle of the road as Sherry ran across in front of him. Screeching up next to her he yelled, "For God's sake, Get in!" Sherry pulled a door open and dove into the sedan barely avoiding a shot fired by Trooper Davis from his position on the ground. With the girl safely in the car Carsten let in the clutch and roared away.

Behind him there was silence except for the groans of the wounded troopers.

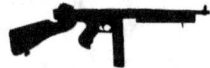

That evening Dan and Larry had a council of war at the St. Louis office of the FBI along with local agents. Dan had driven all day to reach St. Louis by late afternoon. He hadn't checked into a hotel but had gone straight to the Federal building. There Dan briefed Larry on the Indianapolis shootout. Larry shook his head after he heard the details, "You think that was the Wagner girl with Carsten?"

Dan agreed, "I have to believe she was driving Carsten's getaway car." He shook his head, "She must have a crazy idea they're on some kind of romantic adventure."

"More like Bonnie and Clyde, if you ask me," Larry added.

Dan nodded solemnly, "If Carsten is really dying like we think, he won't mind going out in a blaze of glory. And he won't care who he takes with him."

Larry looked thoughtful, "What about the girl?"

Dan grimaced, "She murdered that bodyguard in South Bend. She'll have to answer for that. I guess we try to save her if she lets us. But a lot's going to be up to her." He added, "So what do we have here in town?"

Larry gestured at the other man in the room, "This is agent Dryer. He pointed to a tall, thin agent who nodded in return. He's the agent in charge here in St. Louis. We have Ryan under surveillance. He owns three different businesses here in town. Two dry cleaners and a tailor shop. They're supposedly legitimate but local police suspect that Ryan may be running a numbers operation out of them." While he spoke he pointed at points on a large map of St. Louis pinned to one wall of the office. Dan nodded as Larry continued, "Ryan is living on the fourth floor of the *Columbia Hotel*."

Dan asked, "What? No big mansion in the suburbs?"

Larry shrugged, "Not for him. I guess he figures the service is better in a hotel."

"So what's his schedule?"

"I guess he visits his business most days. Evenings he often goes out on the town with his girlfriend. She lives at the hotel with him, by the way."

Dan winced internally at this news. One more civilian in the line of fire they would have to watch out for. It was painfully obvious that Carsten and his girlfriend didn't care about who they shot down. He spoke up, "We're going to need several teams to watch Ryan's businesses for Carsten. How about it Dryer? How many men have you got available?"

Dryer spoke, "I can put three two man teams on those businesses. I'll lead one team personally."

Dan liked his spirit, "Good. You do that. Larry and I will stay on Ryan. We'll follow him wherever he goes. Hopefully one or more of our teams will be on the spot if and when Carsten shows up."

"What about Duvall in Kanas City," Larry asked?

"I've spoken to our agent in Kansas City. Duvall is thought to be somewhere in the city putting together a new gang. But no one knows exactly where he's holed up. They've got warrants out for him. If he shows up they'll arrest him on sight. Right now I think Ryan is the next name on Carsten's list. St. Louis is closer to Indianapolis and Ryan is out in the public eye where he can be found easily. I think we'll put our chips on this number and let it ride."

Larry nodded the light of battle showing in his eyes.

As the meeting was breaking up an agent came to the doorway and caught Dan's eye. Dan waved him in and took the report he was holding out. He scanned it quickly as the other agents watched with interest. Finally Dan set the report down and grimaced as he looked at the other agents, "We've got a sighting report on Carsten and the girl."

"Good," agent Dryer smiled.

"I'm afraid not," Dan commented. "They shot it out with a couple of State troopers in southern Indiana this afternoon."

Surprised Larry asked, "What happened?"

"It looks like they were stealing a car at a filling station when the troopers happened by. There was a shootout. Both cops are in the hospital. Carsten and the girl got away."

There was silence for a moment then Larry commented sourly, "So she's still with him."

"Worse. She shot one of the officers. They were last seen heading south."

Dryer was angry, "Two more good cops shot. Who do these two think they are?"

Dan looked soberly at the other agents, "They've got nothing got lose. Carsten's dying and this girl thinks she's Bonnie Parker. They're very dangerous. We can't underestimate them." On this sober note the meeting broke up.

The next day Dan and Larry were staked out in the lobby of the *Columbia Hotel*. Dan wanted to speak to Ryan. The *Columbia* was a high class place, and no doubt expensive, but Tommy Ryan was a long time hood and probably had plenty of money stashed. Dan's blood boiled at the thought of a crook like Ryan operating supposedly honest businesses bought with money earned by the crooked rackets he had run over the years.

A short, well dressed, dapper looking man exited one of the elevator cars and into the lobby. Dan caught Larry's eye and stood up. The two G-men accosted Ryan half across the lobby. Dan showed his badge and spoke, "We'd like a word, Ryan."

The racketeer looked sharply at Dan's badge. He seemed about to make a hostile remark but instead plastered a smile on his face and asked, "What can I do for the government this fine morning?" Larry's face darkened but Dan held up a hand to him, "I'd like to know what connection you have to Duke Carsten?"

Ryan was surprised for a moment but recovered well, "Carsten? Sure, I knew Duke Carsten back in Chicago. Seems like I heard he was doing a stretch up in Clarksville." He gave Dan a half smile, "Didn't you G-men put him there?"

Dan nodded, "Yes we did. Unfortunately he's out. You haven't seen him around have you?" Dan looked casual as he asked this but was watching Ryan closely. His shot had gone home. Ryan was clearly surprised at this news; his quick intake of breath was obvious. The hood took a breath and tried to act casual, "Why should he be around here? I haven't seen Duke for years."

Dan nodded and stepped back, "Okay Ryan, thanks for your co-operation." Ryan regained a little of his swagger as he touched the brim of his hat and stepped past the two agents toward the front door of the lobby. Dan let him take three steps toward the revolving door before he said loudly, "You know, they never caught the rest of the gang Duke was running with. They didn't recover any of the money either. That's probably what Duke's looking for."

Ryan stopped in his tracks and visibly stiffened. He turned back toward Dan and said coldly, "You accusing me of something G-man?"

Dan shook his head, "If I had any evidence to accuse you of something we'd already be on our way down to the Federal building. I just thought

"We've got a sighting report on Carsten and the girl."

you ought to know that Duke's out of prison and probably on his way here right now."

"Sure, nice of you to let me know."

He turned to go and Dan added, "I tried to get to Johnny Perucci but I wasn't in time. He's dead now. So is Charlie Nash. He bought the farm up in South Bend a few days ago." In the light of the lobby it was obvious that Ryan's face went a couple shades paler. He gulped and managed to croak out, "Perucci's doing time Indianapolis."

Dan smiled and shook his head, "Not anymore. He was at the Federal courthouse for his trial when Duke Carsten put a couple of slugs in his chest. He got the two policemen who were guarding him as well."

If anything Ryan went even paler. He half whispered, "You're lying!"

"Fraid not. Why I'll bet Duke's probably out there on the street somewhere right now. What do you think Larry?"

Larry nodded and smiled, "Probably got that Tommy gun he was using the other day, Dan. Maybe we ought to call ahead to the morgue and tell them to expect some new business soon."

Ryan brushed past them muttering, "Wise guys!" He headed to a row of phone booths, entered one, closed the folding door behind him and reached for a nickel. Dan motioned to Larry and the two agents went through the revolving door. As they reached the sidewalk Larry laughed, "Well that rattled his cage."

"Yeah, you don't get to see a hood like Ryan that scared very often. Life's just not that fair." They trooped down the street to their car and waited inside. As they did a car pulled up and parked in front of the hotel. The driver sat inside and waited. Ten minutes later another sedan with two men it pulled in behind the first car. Seconds later Ryan scurried out of the hotel and hopped in the first car. It pulled out followed closely by the second car. Larry remarked wryly, "Guess he was listening to you Dan." Dan nodded to Larry and the G-men added their car to the little procession.

They followed Ryan and his men across town to a dry cleaning business. Ryan walked quickly inside followed closely by his driver who must have forgotten his belt that morning because he walked with one hand inside his coat. "Probably holding up his pants," thought Dan with a smile. The second car parked out front; the two men inside looking watchfully around.

Dan and Larry settled in to wait. While they did they took notice of another car with government plates nearby. Two men were also in this vehicle. Larry pointed it out first. Dan said, "Must be on of Dryer's teams; at least we'll have help if Carsten shows up." An hour later Ryan exited the cleaners with is driver and they drove away, followed closely by the two men who had followed them there. He repeated this performance at his other dry cleaning shop.

Ryan's third stop was at his tailor shop. There, two of his men went down the street and brought back what appeared to be food for lunch. This told Dan that the hood was taking Dan's warning seriously. He was limiting his appearances in public. This was just what the agent wanted. When Carsten made his move Dan wanted as few innocent bystanders around as possible. After a couple of hours here, Ryan left in his car with his bodyguards close behind and returned to his hotel. Dan and Larry followed them inside. They saw Ryan safely into his suite. They then checked over the hotel layout and waited through the evening until relieved by other agents. Ryan did not leave his suite for dinner, instead opting to have room service deliver to his room.

The next day followed the same pattern. Dan and Larry followed Ryan as he made his inspections of his businesses. He ate at one of them and returned to the *Columbia Hotel* late in the afternoon. As they pulled up in front of the hotel Ryan was just going inside. The agents hurried inside. Dan spoke to Larry, "Check out the stairwell. I'll follow him up in the elevator. Larry nodded his assent and headed across the lobby. Dan picked up his pace and tried to catch Ryan's elevator. He didn't make it. He watched as Ryan smiled at him cynically as the doors closed. Dan quickly entered the second elevator car and told the operator, "Four, please." The operator nodded, closed the door and sent the elevator upward.

The car slowed and the operator announced, "Fourth floor, sir." The door opened and Dan stepped out reaching into his pocket for a dime to tip the operator. As he did he registered Ryan down the hall opening the door to his suite. A uniformed maid just past him was reaching for clean towels from a cart. Dan reached back to hand the dime to the operator but dropped it as shots rang out in the hallway. Bang! Bang! Bang!

Dan grabbed for his automatic and ducked into the hall. Ryan was down, his arm feebly reaching toward his back. There was blood splattered all over him and the wall. The maid, gun in hand, was fleeing toward the end of the hall. Dan fired once but his bullet hit the maid's abandoned cart. Cursing he ran forward. Getting a clean shot he fired once as the maid dodged into the stairwell but missed. As he ran forward, she leaned out into the hallway and fired her pistol twice. Dan dove to the floor, the bullets passing overhead. He then picked himself up and ran forward. At the stairwell Dan hesitated before kicking it open. The landing was empty but he could hear footsteps from below.

Dan jumped down the steps two at a time, his .45 leading the way. He heard voices and then a door slammed. As it did, gunfire erupted below muffled by the now closed door. "Larry!" Dan yelled. He turned at the last landing and found the ground floor exit in front of him. Dan cautiously pushed open the door with one hand while standing to one side. Silence greeted him. Leaning around the jam he saw a figure down in the hallway. It was Larry. He was leaning against the wall holding a bloody arm as Dan reached him, "I'm alright. It was Carsten. He was waiting on the stairs. He and the girl went that way. " He waved feebly down the hall toward the rear of the building."

Turning Dan yelled at several people clustered near the entrance to the lobby, "We need some help here! An officer's been shot!" As he shouted Larry whispered urgently, "I'll be okay. Go get 'em!" Dan hesitated for a split second whispered, "I'll be back" and ran down the hallway. He immediately came to a large kitchen. Inside chefs and waiters were yelling and helping someone to his feet. Dan yelled, "Federal agent! Clear the way!" brushing past them toward the rear door.

He crashed through the outward opening door into the alley. To his right a car was roaring down the alley, knocking garbage cans and other debris out of the way. Dan braced himself; feet spread and took aim at the fleeing car. He fired and saw the rear window shatter. His second shot opened a hole in the body of the car. Then the fleeing vehicle reached the street, careened into a tight turn, sideswiped a taxi and roared out of Dan's sight.

Running to the mouth of the alley he could see the getaway car weaving through traffic. The driver of the taxi had jumped out of his vehicle and was shaking his fist at the offending sedan while he called the driver an imaginative list of names. Holstering his pistol Dan vaulted across the hood of the taxi and threw himself through the open driver's door. As he rammed the car into gear the driver turned and yelled, "Hey, what are you . . ." His final words were drowned out by the screeching of tires as Dan floored the taxis' accelerator.

Weaving through the heavy, late afternoon traffic Dan couldn't see the car Carsten had fled in. He cut in front of a bus, clipped the bumper of another taxi earning an angry blast from its horn and then ran a red light. Barely avoiding disaster in the intersection he soon caught sight of the fleeing sedan. It too was ignoring traffic laws as it fled at high speed.

Finally reaching an open area Dan gunned the taxi forward. He was now only one car behind the big sedan. Leaning on the horn he waved with his free hand attempting to get the driver ahead to pull over. At the first the driver just angrily waved Dan around him. Afraid that Carsten would speed away while Dan was stuck behind the slower auto, Dan wrenched the wheel to the left to pass it when the car swerved wildly to the curb with a squeal of brakes.

Nonplussed Dan was at a loss for a moment until he realized the car had swerved away because an arm holding a gun had emerged from the rear driver side window of the fleeing sedan. Dan ducked and jerked the wheel to the right as flame bloomed from the muzzle of the gangster's weapon. Head low, Dan felt glass rain over his head and shoulders as the windshield shattered. He could feel the big slugs tear into the metal body of the taxi as well.

Sitting up he pressed the accelerator down as he peered between the cracks and scarring of the windshield. Wind whistled around him through the holes the bullets had made. Knowing that Carsten must be reloading Dan pushed the cab forward. Alone, he couldn't use his weapon as he would have liked. Instead he intended to force the sedan off the road. Once the cars were stopped he would have the advantage.

Accelerating forward he rammed the rear bumper of the sedan with a clang. The impact was not great but hopefully it would keep the two felons off balance. The girl was obviously driving; perhaps he could force her to lose control. Swerving outwards Dan tried to ram the left rear fender. As he connected with the sedan he saw Carsten's face at the rear window gun in hand. Dan braked hard to get out of the line of fire as Carsten opened up once more. Gritting his teeth Dan twisted his left hand back and under his arm. Getting his automatic out he reached out the driver's window the pistol grasped in his left hand. He wasn't a great shot with his off-hand but he couldn't let Carsten turn the cab into Swiss cheese. As he took aim across the hood Dan noticed steam coming from under the hood. Cursing he fired once and then again as the steam rapidly increased. Then the engine began to falter. Dan watched helplessly as the battered sedan pulled rapidly away. With the engine threatening to seize up he reluctantly pulled the damaged taxi to the curb. He got out holstering his automatic and kicked a tire in frustration.

Dan waited impatiently until a St. Louis police car pulled up next to him. Identifying himself he gave him a report and hitched a ride back to the *Columbia*. All was chaos there. Uniformed police and detectives were everywhere. As Dan crossed the lobby a sheet covered body was carried past him. He quickly found agent Dryer who he questioned about Larry. The agent replied, "He took a slug to the arm. I think he's going to be okay. He was talking as they put him in the ambulance."

Relieved, Dan let out the breath he had been holding, "Did he say anything about Carsten?"

Dryer nodded, "He said Carsten was as surprised as he was when he burst out the stairway door. He's also pretty sure he clipped Carsten. He's not sure how bad." Dan thanked the agent and went across the lobby to examine where Larry's fight had taken place. He carefully scouted the hallway and kitchen of the hotel. Sure enough he found spots of blood leading to the alley. Larry had indeed hit Carsten. How bad the man was hit was another question?

Dan quickly put out an alert to all law enforcement that Carsten and his girlfriend were on the loose in St. Louis. He also had local police alert all doctors and hospitals that Carsten was wounded and might seek care. He then headed to the hospital to check on Larry's condition. The doctor there assured him that Larry's wound wasn't that serious. He would be out of the hospital in a few days.

From there Dan went downtown to the Federal building. There he was speaking to Agent Dryer about borrowing some of his men when an agent stuck his head into the office, "Agent Fowler? The director is on the line for you."

Dryer raised an eyebrow and pointed to the phone on his desk, "You can take it here." He then left the office discreetly.

Dan sat down behind the desk and picked up the receiver, "Yes director, this is Fowler."

"I've been following reports from the Midwest offices. Anything positive to report?"

"No sir, I pursued Carsten after the shooting here but I'm afraid he got away again."

Dan clearly heard the crash of the director's fist hitting something hard, probably his desk, "Blast it Fowler. This hood is running amok across three states! He's making law enforcement look like monkeys!"

Dan held the receiver away from his ear as he leaned toward the candle stick phone, "Yes sir, I'm afraid you're right. But I assure you every man is working hard to bring Carsten and his girlfriend to justice. Larry Kendal was shot today in a gunfight with Carsten."

There was a slight pause and the director's voice came back more calmly, "The Indianapolis courthouse shooting was bad enough, but now this. I don't have to tell you how much play this story is getting in the newspapers Fowler. We need to get Carsten soon before law enforcement gets a bigger black eye than it already has. Am I clear?"

"Yes sir, very clear."

The director cleared his throat before adding, "Dan you're the best there is, and you're my good right arm. You have my full confidence. If there's anything you need call at once."

"Thank you, sir. Everyone here will do their best."

"I have no doubt. How is young Kendal?"

"Wounded sir, but he's going to be alright."

"Good. Carry on." Dan thanked the Director and hung up. The pressure was certainly on. He rubbed his jaw in concentration. He knew where Carsten would go next. He intended to be there, ready and waiting, when he arrived.

Two hours after the shootout in St. Louis a Sedan drifted to a stop in a small town just outside Columbia Missouri. A young girl jumped out closed her door and leaned through the rear window, "I'll be right back, Duke."

The shadowy figure leaning back in the rear seat spoke, "Be quick about it baby; in and out just like I showed you."

She smiled at him and quickly turned to enter the drug store. Inside she looked around carefully. There was young soda jerk making up a treat for a teenage girl at the soda fountain. The only other person visible was the druggist standing at the cash register. He looked at her inquiringly but she just smiled and turned down an aisle searching for the items she wanted.

Three minutes later she dumped her purchases on the counter. The druggist sorted through them, "Let's see; gauze, bandages, alcohol . . ." he frowned at her, "Looks like someone's been hurt."

Reaching into her purse the girl came up with her automatic and pointed it at the astonished druggist's face, "You better hope he's the only one Pops. Now put everything a bag. Empty the cash register while you're at it." Keeping her eyes on the druggist, she pointed down the counter to the soda fountain, "You two just sit still and nobody gets hurt." The young girl turned pale but said nothing, the soda jerk stood frozen in place a scoop of ice cream in one hand, a glass in the other.

A minute later the young bandit stepped out onto the sidewalk. She held up the bag she was holding and waved at the sedan. She then turned and walked two doors down to a restaurant. As she entered a waiter stepped up to her and asked with a smile, "Would you like a table, Miss?"

She again produced her pistol and replied, "No thanks, but I need something to go." Two minutes later she ran out of the restaurant waving a bottle of champagne. Moments later the sedan accelerated away with a screech of tires. A girl's wild laughter was heard by a man walking past on the sidewalk.

The next morning Dan stepped off a train onto the platform in the Kansas City railway station. He had telegraphed ahead the night before and expected to be met by bureau operatives. He wasn't disappointed. A stocky redhead man in a conservative suit stepped up to him, "Fowler? I'm agent Baker."

Dan held out his hand, "Thanks for meeting me Baker. Is everything lined up?"

The other agent nodded as he led Dan toward the street doors, "Yes sir, I've spoken to Washington and they briefed me. You're to have anything you need."

"Are your men lined up?"

"Yes. They're waiting downtown for you now. I take it you have a plan?"

Dan nodded, "I do. I'll brief your men and we'll get started right away. For all we know Carsten may be in town already."

"If we don't know where to find Duvall, how can Carsten find him?"

"He may not know where Duvall is now. But knowing Carsten and how determined he is. I have to believe he'll find him soon enough."

Agent Baker nodded as steered the bureau car downtown to the Federal building. Once there he led Dan to a large office where the local agents were gathered. Dan nodded to a couple of agents that he knew personally as he stepped to the front of the room. Once there he got right to business, "As you all know we missed Carsten in St. Louis. We had staked out all of Ryan's hangouts expecting Carsten to try for Ryan out in the open. Unfortunately, he got the drop on us by using his girlfriend. She was disguised as a maid and killed Ryan while he was entering his hotel room." There was a stir from the agents at this revelation. Before he could continue, one agent raised his hand and spoke, "So this girl isn't just an innocent along for the ride?"

Dan shook his head, "No. She is as dangerous as Carsten. We don't understand her motives for playing along with him; maybe it's just for kicks. But she is a full and willing participant. Be extremely careful. She will undoubtedly be armed and is not afraid to shoot."

"Now, as I was saying St. Louis didn't work out so we're going to try something different here. We're going to search out Duvall before Carsten can find him. Then we're going to use him as bait to lure Carsten in. That way Carsten and the girl will come to us. So far Carsten and his girl have set the battlefields. This time we will. Any questions?"

There were several. The first came from Baker, "What's your plan for finding Duvall?"

Dan smiled, "That's where you local agents come in. You know the ground and players. I want you to spread out and in conjunction with local police start squeezing every stoolie and informant you can find. If Duvall has been operating in this area; somebody must know where he can be found. We'll follow up all leads and sooner or later we'll get him."

The rest of the questions were minor and soon the meeting broke up and the agents headed for the streets looking for info. Dan smiled. He was confident this new method would finally put him ahead of Carsten. This time would be their final battle.

Duke Carsten and Sherry were holed up in a motor court just outside Kansas City. A late model La Salle, recently stolen, was parked behind the cabin. Inside Duke sat on the bed, his shirt off. Sherry Wagner finished wrapping a bandage around his torso and stepped back. Duke nodded, "That's good. Gimme that bottle will ya baby."

The girl smiled and swayed across the room to the beat up wooden dresser. She was dressed in a white nylon slip and little else. Picking up an open bottle of whiskey and a corked bottle of champagne she crossed back to the bed. She handed the whiskey bottle to Duke who moved gingerly back onto the bed reclining against the wall. He took a swig from the bottle and watched while Sherry worked at the champagne cork. It finally came loose with a loud "Pop!" Immediately the bottle foamed over onto her hand and arm. She laughed and raised the bottle to her lips. She took a long drink, the foam running down her cheeks as Duke watched languidly.

She lowered the bottle and wiped her lips with the back of her free hand and giggled, "That tickles my nose!" She then flounced over to the bed to lie down on her stomach looking at Duke, "So when are we gonna move Duke?"

Duke took another swig from the bottle and said thoughtfully, "Couple of days. I'll be healed up pretty soon and we need to let the heat die down."

Sherry drank from the champagne bottle and asked, "What do we do after we get the last one?"

Duke shrugged, "Whatever you want."

She giggled, "I wanna travel. I wanna see New York, San Francisco…we can travel can't we Duke? I mean, we have money now and after we finish this guy we'll have lots of time to see everything, right Duke?"

Duke took another drink from the bottle and not looking at the girl nodded, "Sure Doll. We got lots of time."

The Federal Agents spread out all over town and for the next two days rousted anyone they thought might have the slightest connection to Frank Duvall. Dan monitored their efforts and interrogated the most promising ones himself. Duvall was definitely operating in the Kansas City area. Many people had seen him but no one knew where he was hiding out or if they did, they weren't talking.

On the evening of the second day agent Baker leaned into the office Dan was working out of and announced, "Dan, we've got a live one you might want to have a go at."

Dan stood up, "Good. We've got to find Duvall soon. Carsten is around here somewhere I can feel it. If we don't find Duvall before Carsten does there'll be blood in the streets." The two agents went down a floor and ended up in front of a door marked *Interrogation*. Inside was a thin, rather pale,

She took a long drink, the foam running down her cheeks...

middle aged man in shirt sleeves. His tie was loosened and he squinted against the glare of a bright light focused on him.

Agent Baker spoke to Dan, "This is Ace Tegowski. We picked him up at a garage he runs. He sells cars to anybody, no questions asked. There were nearly a dozen cars in his garage with plates from five different states. We're running the plates now but five'll get you ten most of them are stolen."

The man squinted at Baker and held up a hand attempting to see behind the bright light, "Hey, I know my rights! Stolen cars aren't a federal beef! You got no right to hold me!"

Dan stepped forward, "Well Ace, normally you'd be right. Unfortunately for you that many cars could mean you're transporting stolen autos across state lines. That could easily be interpreted as a federal offense." He paused for a moment, "Of course that could mean time in a federal prison."

Ace looked uncomfortable. In fact he was sweating profusely. Dan thought wryly to himself that it might be from the hot lights but probably not. He pulled out a chair and dropped into it across from the unfortunate man. Ace could make his form out but Dan was still comfortably in shadow. He stuttered, "Loo. . . look, that ain't gonna stand up. I just buy used cars and fix 'em up. I don't know where they come from."

Dan smiled even though his prisoner couldn't see it, "We'll see soon enough. Those registrations will be coming through soon. While we wait though, maybe you could help us out." He paused dramatically, "If you co-operated maybe we could work something out with the DA."

Squinting, Ace looked suspiciously past the light, "Yeah, like how?"

Dan and Baker exchanged a look before Baker spoke, "The word is you run a poker game at your garage on weekends Ace. We know Frank Duvall is in town. He likes to gamble and is flush lately, if you've seen him that might be worth something."

Ace fidgeted for a bit before tentatively saying, "Yeah, I might have seen Duvall around."

"Okay. So where's he holed up at?"

"Look, he just shows up to play. I don't know where he's hiding out." He paused, "He might be around next Saturday night though."

Dan exchanged a look with Baker, "That's too late. We need to find Duvall today. If you can't help us then you're going down for everything we can throw at you."

Ace licked his lips and finally shook his head, "I don't know for sure but I hear he's hangin' out at Mollie's at the *Gateway Hotel*. She runs some girls out of the top floor. Dan exchanged a glance with Baker at this news. Baker nodded imperceptibly. Dan looked back to Ace, "Okay Ace, We'll check it out. If you're telling the truth we'll take it into account. Meanwhile you're gonna be the government's guest for a while." He nodded and an agent grabbed Ace by the arm. The hoodlum squirmed, "Hey, that's not right! I told you everything I know!" Dan was silent as the agent dragged Ace out of the room. He then turned to Agent Baker, "What do you think?"

"I think we should have a talk with Mollie. If Duvall's there we need to take him quietly."

Dan nodded, "Right. We don't want to tip off Carsten." Dan and Baker left the interrogation room together.

The next day Dan, Baker and two other agents stood in the stairwell leading to the top floor of the Gateway Hotel. They were checking their weapons when a plain clothes St. Louis detective entered the stairwell. He spoke in a low voice, "The floor's clear. Mollie has moved all her girls out along with customers. Duvall is in 516 at the end of the hall." He hesitated a moment before adding, "There's a girl with him."

Dan turned to the other agents, "We'll go in hard. Nobody shoots unless it's absolutely necessary. Hopefully we'll catch him with his pants down." There were several grins at this remark. Dan continued seriously, "Watch your fire. The girl's just trying to earn a dollar. We want to keep this as quiet as possible so we bring Duvall down the back stairwell. Gag him if you have to. Everybody clear?"

There were nods all around. The four agents left the stairwell quickly and moved silently down the hallway guns drawn. When they reached room 516, Dan and two others spread themselves to each side of the door. The largest agent stood across from it. Dan looked around one final time and nodded at the big agent. He took two strides across the hall and hit the door with the sole of his shoe just above the door knob. The door flew open with a crash. Dan immediately led the other two agents into the room. A dark haired man was lying in bed. A young girl wearing practically nothing screamed and rolled off the bed trying to cover herself with a blanket she pulled after her. The dark haired man reached toward a revolver hanging in a holster on the brass bedstead but froze as Dan barked out, "Don't try it Duvall! You won't make it!"

Reluctantly the man turned back and raised his hands. Dan nodded and two of the agents moved forward. In seconds Duvall was cuffed and gagged with a towel. In his underwear he was escorted to the stairwell. Dan took a moment with a local police detective, "Take the girl in. Hold her on a morals charge for a few days. After this is over, turn her loose. Remember she is not to talk to anyone." The detective saluted and entered the room to take the crying girl into custody. Dan holstered his weapon and followed his men down the stairs.

Dan started the stakeout that night. There were two agents in Duvall's room at all times. Two others had the room next door. More agents were in nearby cars and an agent was staking out the lobby. Madam Mollie had not wanted to co-operate but she had come around after the correct persuasion had been applied by the District Attorney and the St. Louis Chief of Detectives. She was again running a few of her girls but they were clustered in rooms at the other end of the floor. She had been briefed to watch out for Carsten and the Wagner girl.

The next morning Dan got a pleasant surprise when Larry Kendal walked into his office in the Federal building. He had his left arm in a sling but otherwise looked his usual cheerful self. Dan got up and came forward hand outstretched, "Larry! It's good to see you. How's the arm?"

As Larry shook Dan's hand he shrugged, "Not bad. The Doc's say it's healing cleanly. I just have to put up with this sling for a few more days."

Dan smiled, "How's your gun arm?"

Larry held up his right hand and wiggled his fingers, "Good enough to help you take on Carsten. I owe him one, remember?"

Dan replied, "I haven't forgotten. He's slipped through our fingers for the last time. This time he'll be coming to us."

"So I hear. You got Duvall and haven't told anyone?"

"Right. We spread word around on the street that he's hiding out at the *Gateway Hotel*. Sooner or later Carsten will show up there. When he does we'll be waiting."

Larry nodded, "That's for me. Are you heading over there soon?"

"Soon enough. First we're going to check in with the locals to see if any of their informants have heard anything. We'll take up the stakeout later."

Dan and Larry took over inside 516 that afternoon. While they kept watch Dan brought Larry up to date on everything that had happened since he had been shot. Larry approved of Dan's plans to get ahead of Carsten and his girlfriend. He frowned when her name came up though, "I don't like the idea of throwing down on a girl, Dan. She should be out on dates with boys her age not running with a killer like Carsten."

Dan shook his head, "It's a tough situation Larry, but we can't underestimate her. She didn't hesitate to gun down Tommy Ryan. And she was throwing lead at me as well. We should keep that in mind when they show up. At this point she's as dangerous as Carsten is." He hesitated a moment before adding, "Maybe more dangerous. A lot of lawmen will hesitate before throwing down on her. That could cost somebody his life."

The evening passed without any sign of Carsten. Dan and Larry were relieved by other agents. The next day Dan was impatient. He was tying up a lot of manpower. He couldn't maintain this level of stakeout for long. He remarked as much to Larry when they again relieved two agents the next afternoon in Room 516. Larry agreed, "You're right Dan. The director's going to want results and soon."

Dan shook his head, "I was on the phone to him this morning. He's getting impatient alright." Larry nodded soberly. He was about to say something else when there was a sharp knock on the door. Both agents went for their guns but relaxed when a voice came through the door, "Agent Fowler! The girl's here!"

Dan wrenched the room door open as he re-holstered his automatic, "Where is she?"

The agent who had been stationed in the lobby stood before him, "I saw the Wagner girl come in to the lobby. She went to the desk and asked for something. The clerk then made a call. A couple of minutes later Mollie came down to meet her. The two were talking so I beat it up here."

"Any sign of Carsten?"

"No sir."

Dan chewed his lip for a moment, "Go back down and keep an eye on the girl. Stay alert. She may be scouting for Carsten or she may come up here herself to try for Duvall. Remember she's probably armed."

"Right." The agent hurried away. Dan turned to find Larry up against the wall next to the window overlooking the street. He held the drape slightly outward so he could see below. A few moments later he looked Dan's way, "There she goes, Dan. Going down the sidewalk to the right."

Making a quick decision Dan yelled, "Let's go!" and turned for the door. Dan ran down the hall with Larry close on his heels. Ignoring the elevator the two agents made for the stairs. There they jumped down three steps at a time. Less than a minute later they banged out the stairway door into the lobby, guns up. The lobby agent waved them toward the front door yelling, "The girl went that way!" He fell into step with Dan as they all ran across the lobby, "The girl was in here pretending to look for a job with the madam."

As they crashed through the front door onto the sidewalk Dan asked, "Do you think she spotted you?" The agent shook his head, "I don't think so." Dan caught sight of one of the bureau cars parked down the street and waved them forward. Dan ran around to the driver's side and pulled open the door, "I'm driving. Get in the back!" The agent behind the wheel obeyed and piled in next to Larry.

With everybody inside Dan shoved the car into gear and accelerated down the street. Dan called out, "The girl is on this street. Keep an eye out for her." The other agents nodded as they checked their weapons. The agent in back had grabbed a tommy gun stowed there. Larry on the other side of the back seat had pulled his automatic as had the agent next to Dan.

Dan weaved around traffic as they entered the next block. Suddenly the agent next to him yelled out, "There she is! She's getting in a car." Sure enough ahead the Wagner girl was just climbing into a big blue Cadillac Sedan. Once inside it pulled into traffic and drove slowly away. Dan slowed and fell in several cars behind the big Caddy. He spoke tersely to the other agents, "Anybody get a look at the driver? Was it Duke?"

There were negative responses from the other agents. They continued through the streets at a leisurely pace for a few minutes before Larry asked, "Where are they going?"

"Back to their hideout," one of the other agents put in.

"They're sure not in a hurry, are they?" Larry asked.

As Larry spoke Dan realized that Carsten was looking for a tail. Instinctively he slowed the bureau car attempting to drop a back a bit. Too late, the Cadillac sped up, swerved around a taxi and screeched around the next corner. "I guess they've seen us," Dan yelled as he pressed the accelerator down. The same taxi slowed him and he was forced to brake hard while it got out of his way. He then shot off down the side street after the Cadillac. Ahead he saw it making a left onto another street. He followed.

The Cadillac was powerful and the agents' car was heavily loaded. They were not gaining. Traffic was heavy. Ahead Dan saw the Cadillac swerve around a trolley car narrowly missing two oncoming cars. He kept the accelerator down though hoping for a break. He got it at the next intersection. The signal turned red. The Cadillac slowed to avoid a vehicle crossing in front of it then accelerated across the intersection. It almost made it; another car clipped its rear bumper sending it into a slide. It jumped the sidewalk and clipped two parking meters as the driver tried to get it under control.

The agents cheered as Dan closed the gap. At a range of fifty feet the rear window of the Cadillac shattered. Flashes came from within the big car. The agent next to Dan swore as a slug hit their windshield starring it. Dan ducked down and yelled out, "Better slow 'em down a little!" The agent leaned out the passenger window and fired across the hood at the fleeing auto.

Ahead the Cadillac swerved right around a slower auto and careened into a right turn. It was going too fast and rose up on two wheels. It probably would have rolled over but halfway through the turn it sideswiped a produce truck that threw it back onto four wheels. Dan slammed on the brakes and cranked the steering wheel to the right as he followed the Cadillac into the turn.

Straightening up the agents' car was now about twenty yards behind the fleeing car when again bright flashes came from the shattered rear window of the car ahead. Dan yelled, "Duck!" He scrunched down behind the wheel as the windshield above his head was hit multiple times and shattered. There yells of surprise and pain around him. Glass flew everywhere as noise and wind filled the car.

Dan raised his head and peered through a hole in the windshield. Squinting against the wind he saw they had fallen back and he again pressed the accelerator to the floor. As he did he called out, "Anybody hurt?" Amid the curses Larry yelled, "We're okay, Dan. Jenkins got nicked but he's alright. Before Dan could reply to this the agent next to him turned around in his seat and shouted, "Pass that Tommy gun up here!"

The gun was quickly passed over the seat as Dan continued to steer after their quarry. Ahead the Cadillac was forced to brake for traffic. As the agent's car closed on their quarry the Cadillac swerved right onto the sidewalk and shot forward. Dan swerved to the left around a nearly stopped taxi leaning on his horn as he did. They passed it and were diagonally behind and to the left of the Cadillac as it roared down the sidewalk, pedestrians jumping frantically out of its way.

Dan's ears were assaulted by the sound of gunfire as the agent next to him and Larry behind him fired out their windows at the Cadillac. Bullets slammed into the big car. Dan saw two of its windows shatter. Dan tried to yell at them to fire at the tires but his shouts were drowned out by the roar of their guns. One of them must have heard or perhaps it was just luck but the left front tire on the Cadillac was shot out. Instantly the big car swerved hard to the left back into the street. It sideswiped a car, shot across the opposite sidewalk and plowed through the plate glass window of a restaurant.

Dan jumped on the brake with both feet. The agent's car screeched to a stop at the end of a trail of burnt rubber on the pavement. Amazed shouts came from those around him.

"Wow!"

"Did you see that?"

"Cripes!"

Turning in his seat Dan saw people streaming out of the restaurant, some of them climbing out the smashed window and past the rear trunk of the Cadillac, which was all that was visible of the big car. Jerking on the gear shift lever, Dan rammed the transmission into reverse and roared back eighty feet until they were opposite the violated restaurant. There the agents piled out of the car. Gunfire and screams came from inside the battered building.

Taking cover behind the hood of their car Dan took stock of the situation. Pedestrians were fleeing into nearby businesses or down the street. Traffic had stopped. Some drivers were getting out of their cars to see what was going on. More people were leaning out of windows for the same reason. Larry was just behind him yelling at the top of his lungs, "This is the FBI! Everybody stay back! Take cover!" No one seemed to be listening until a burst of automatic fire came from the restaurant. That encouraged everyone still standing in the street to duck or flee. Sirens growing louder were all around them.

Dan pointed at the two agents with him, both now held Tommy guns,

"You guys go right and left. Hold your fire until my order."

They nodded and ducked away from the car running crouched. Both found cover behind nearby autos and covered the restaurant with their weapons. Larry moved up next to Dan, his .45 in his hand, "What now, Dan?"

Dan held his reply for a moment until the deafening siren of an arriving police car wound down. Out of the car jumped four uniformed police officers. Before Dan could wave them to cover, more gunfire strongly encouraged them to do just that. Dan looked at Larry and smiled grimly, "It probably won't do much good but now we talk."

He cupped his hands around his mouth and shouted at the restaurant, "Carsten! It's all over Carsten! You're surrounded! Come out with your hands up! No one has to die today!"

There was a moment of quiet and then gunfire erupted from the restaurant. Single shots followed by automatic fire. Dan reluctantly yelled out, "Fire!"

The Federal agents and police officers immediately cut loose with their weapons. Gunfire poured into the shattered building and car. It went on for several seconds then faded as Dan waved and shouted for a pause.

The sudden quiet was deafening. Smoke was beginning to drift out of the destroyed front window. Something in the restaurant's kitchen must have caught fire. More police were arriving. Uniformed officers carrying riot guns and submachine guns fanned out to surround the restaurant. Dan yelled once again, "Come on out Carsten. This is your last chance!"

Gunfire again answered him. This time he didn't have time to give a command. Police immediately showered the damaged business. Dan didn't even bother to fire. There were so many bullets flying around that he ducked to avoid ricochets. Again there was a pause. The crackling of flames was now added to the growing clouds of smoke belching from the restaurant. Through the smoke Dan thought he saw movement. Larry saw it too. He nudged Dan, "What's that?"

Before Dan could reply a figure materialized in the window crouched next to the bullet riddled Cadillac. The figure jumped down onto the sidewalk and ran forward spraying bullets from the Tommy gun it held. Immediately the street was filed with the roar of police and Federal agents weapons. The figure was cut down in literally a hail of bullets. Dan's shouts of, "Ceasefire!" were drowned out. Soon the gunfire died of its own accord.

Dan stood up and moved around the hood of the car, Larry at his side. The two agents cautiously approached the unmoving figure sprawled in the street. They reached the blood stained figure and stared down. Dan didn't hear the commotion around him as police and firemen ran forward to the burning restaurant. He holstered his pistol as Larry spoke in a hushed voice, "It's the girl, Dan." Dan said nothing as he thrust his pistol back in its holster. Larry was staring down at the still figure. He looked at Dan with sad eyes, "What a waste. Why'd she do it?"

Dan shook his head sadly, "I wish I had an answer Larry. At least it's over now."

"Hey, here's Carsten!" one of the uniform officers called out from inside the demolished restaurant. Dan couldn't even see the cop, the smoke being so heavy. "Or what's left of him," came the final verdict.

Dan Fowler turned away and walked toward their car leaving Larry staring sadly at the unmoving figure. He had a report to make.

The End

Writing Dead Man Shooting

*D*ead Man Shooting had a simple genesis; its birth was more difficult. A year ago I was between active writing assignments. At any one time I am usually working on several writing involved activities at once. I might be outlining one story at the same time I am writing a second story while simultaneously proofreading or revising a submitted manuscript. This is totally normal for me.

If I'm writing something and get a sudden great idea for a new story or novel, I stop everything to get it down on paper before I lose it. This might just be a several paragraph synopsis or it might be a two thousand word outline. Meanwhile current projects continue. If an editor wants that proofreading done so he can go to print with a book then I have to respond promptly. This has gotten to be quite normal for me and more than one professional writer has told me of similar experiences. So last year I found myself not very busy. I was outlining a longer story that hopefully will be seeing the light of day soon, but other than that wasn't doing much.

Since it felt a little strange to not have a bunch of things going on at once I cast around for new projects. While looking through an Airship 27 update I saw that Ron was looking to do a new volume of Dan Fowler G-man stories. I had only a vague knowledge of Dan Fowler but I knew he was one of the longest running pulp heroes so I decided to take a closer look.

I scouted through my pulp library and found a half dozen of the ace G-man's adventures and read them. They weren't bad. Some I liked more than others. *G-Men* magazine was published for a long time and written by a lot of different writers. Dan Fowler sounded like he would be worth writing about. The Fowler stories ranged from '30s gangsters through Axis saboteurs to post war organized crime stories. So the first thing to do was decide was which time period I would set my story in. I consulted with Ron and we agreed that the '30s gang busting stories would be more fun so that's what I chose.

The next thing was a plot. I had a couple of vague ideas but when I talked to Ron he came up with a suggestion that we both thought was great. Ron said he would love to see a story about a terminally ill gangster released from prison who sets out to revenge himself on his former gang. Essentially he would be on a one way trip, sort of a death ride. It sounded like a formula for a fast moving story with lots of action. I can't remember if Ron suggested having a girlfriend along or if she just came up naturally during the writing but she eventually took on a bigger role in the story.

So with a good plot off I went. At first the writing went fine. The story progressed as Ron and I had discussed. As expected there was lots of action. Unfortunately several thousand words into the story I realized two things. One; the story was quite dark. And two; the story was strangely colorless. I decided it need more personality so I came up several scenes showing the other side of the story as told from the fugitive's point of view. This helped. It added both color and length.

Unfortunately the story still didn't seem to have much personality. It was also still dark and violent. So I took a break and thought about the problem. Finally I realized that Dan Fowler is not really my kind of hero. He is a cop. He has no secret identity, no personal life to speak of or interesting motivations. He is essentially a government gunman. I'm afraid I prefer more colorful heroes, especially my pulp heroes. This wasn't too much of a surprise. I've always loved the masked heroes of the '30s and '40s; probably because they were colorful and bigger than life. Still I had made a commitment and I had a lot invested in this story. I wanted it to work so I went back to the keyboard.

A while back a good friend told me that not all stories come out the way you conceive them. I realized there is a lot of wisdom in that. Stories do take on a life of their own. I realized that *Dead Man Shooting* was going to be a gangbusters style action piece and nothing would change that. It didn't have as much personality as I would have liked but that wasn't necessarily bad. A lot of the gangster pulps of the '30s were quite violent. So I let the violence stand but went back and added some flourishes and some bits of interesting dialogue to give the story a little more color. That helped too.

In the end the story you have just read had a difficult gestation but it is alive and well and I believe it will be a good addition to this latest volume of Dan Fowler's adventures. I worked hard on *Dead Man Shooting* and am proud of the results. It is a little bit different from my usual work but Dan Fowler is a different hero than the ones I usually write about. That's okay. It never hurts to step out of your comfort zone and try something new.

A big thank you goes to Ron Fortier for this project. He came up with the basic story idea and helped me along the way with much good advice. I hope you like *Dead Man Shooting*. It was a lot of work but it is good to see it in print.

GENE MOYERS - studied European and Medieval history at the University of Oregon. He is also a U.S. Army veteran. He worked in the high tech industry for some time and ran a store front and internet hobby shop for several years. An avid military gamer and role player, his favorite game was *Daredevils* a pulp based roleplaying game set in the 1930s. His love affair with the 1930s and pulps in particular stem from his first time reading a *Shadow* novel as a boy. Although interested in writing since a teen he did not turn to serious writing until 2000.

He is the co-author of *GURPS Crusades* published by Steve Jackson Games. He has now written several stories for Airship 27 including stories published in *Ravenwood vol. 2, The Purple Scar vol. 1, The Domino Lady vol. 1, Black Bat vol. 3, The Phantom Detective vol. 1* and *The Legends of New Pulp Fiction.* He has also written soon to be published stories for both Moonstone Books and Pro Se Press. When not working on various new pulp projects he is busy writing horror adventures for his colonial swashbuckler. Gene currently lives in Beaverton Oregon with his wife and two lazy dogs.

THE MASK OF MESUD

by Aaron Powers

Dan Fowler set his fork down on the scraps of a healthy serving of scrambled eggs, bacon, and toast, as Sally Vane slid her petite figure into the seat across from him in the diner booth. Sally pulled her heavy brown coat off her shoulders and brushed her shoulder-length blonde hair away from her face. She wore a deep green dress that complemented her small frame, her light skin standing out in contrast to the dark blue booth in which she sat. Dan took a drag from the cigarette in his right hand as he watched her, leaning his broad-shouldered frame against the back of the booth. He had a rugged, somewhat craggy complexion, and was wearing a black suit with a white dress shirt and black tie; the edge of his shoulder holster that held a .357 blue steel revolver peeked out from behind his lapel. The half-full cup of hot coffee on the table had steam rising from the top, fogging up the diner window that had a fresh coat of frost clinging to the exterior.

"Good morning, Dan," remarked Sally, her cornflower blue eyes sparkling as she produced her own cigarette and lit it with her pearl-inlay lighter.

"Good morning, Sally," replied Dan with a smile. He ran a hand through his dark hair.

"Sure is cold out there," continued Sally, "even for the first week of December." She drew from her cigarette, held it, and slowly exhaled.

Dan deposited his cigarette into the ashtray and reached for his coffee.

"D.C. can be a chilly place this time of year, which is why I come to Millie's every day for a hot breakfast and an even hotter cup of coffee." He took a healthy sip and set the cup on the table.

Sally ashed her cigarette and returned it to her ruby red lips, still holding it between her alabaster fingers topped with nail polish that matched her mouth.

"We have the briefing about the new attaché from Germany this morning," she said before taking another drag. "Chief wants us in his office by nine o'clock sharp."

Dan glanced at the silver watch on his left wrist. The hands showed him that it was a quarter past eight.

"Well, just enough time to finish my coffee. Any for you, my dear?"

"No thanks. I had my cup at home."

Dan picked up his coffee cup and drank what was left. Wiping his mouth with his napkin, he reached into his jacket and pulled out his wallet. Depositing a crisp dollar bill on the table, he reached for his coat next to him in the booth.

"Shall we?" he said, standing up and pulling on his coat.

"Very well," replied Sally as she stood, holding her coat. "Up for a walk?"

"Why not?" said Dan as helped her put on her coat. "It's a good morning for a walk, and the Bureau is only a few blocks."

"Sounds good," Sally responded. "Lead the way, Mr. Fowler!"

Dan and Sally walked down the sidewalk, Sally's left arm linked through Dan's right elbow. Their breath puffed out before them as people bustled by on their way to work.

"I can't believe 1935 is almost at an end," remarked Sally as they waited at a busy intersection.

"Me neither," replied Dan, watching as the last car drove by before stepping out into the street. "And with it, I'll be another year closer to thirty."

Sally swatted at him playfully as they passed a woman who was hanging garland on her wrought iron fence. "You don't look a day over twenty-seven."

Dan threw his head back and let out a full laugh in reaction to the mirth of Sally's comment.

"Why, thank you, Sally. And I'll always have you around to keep me young."

Sally laughed in return, hers more musical than Dan's. "For now, Mr. Fowler, but until you buy me that perfect spot of land out west, I'm going to be a city girl."

Dan chuckled as they reached the steps of the Department of Justice building. On either side of the entrance, the bronze seal of the Federal Bureau of Investigation, an eagle with its wings spread wide, shone brilliantly in the morning sun.

Dan held the door open for Sally as they entered. Each produced their badge for the security guard standing inside the entrance.

"Good morning, Agent Fowler. Good morning, Agent Vane," remarked the security guard, a man in his early fifties.

"Good morning, Bert," replied Dan. "How's the hip?"

"Hurts in this cold, that's for sure," said Bert.

"A warm cup of tea and a comfy chair is the remedy for that," commented Sally as she took off her coat and slung it over her arm.

"With one or two shots of whiskey!" winked Bert in reply.

Sally gave another musical laugh as she and Dan walked to the bank of elevators. They waited with a few others while the closest elevator returned to the ground floor. As soon as the exterior door opened, the elevator operator, a boy of about seventeen wearing a red bellhop's uniform, opened the interior gate and five people rushed out. As soon as they were clear, Dan, Sally, and those they were waiting with entered. Dan waited until the others had announced their desired floors before telling the operator to take them to the seventh floor.

Upon reaching the seventh floor, Dan and Sally, along with the operator, were the only ones still in the elevator. The lift came to a stop, and the operator pulled back the gate as the exterior door opened.

"Good day, sir. Good day, ma'am," said the elevator operator, touching his cap.

"Have a good day, Ernie," smiled Sally, brushing his arm with her hand. Ernie turned as red as his outfit before he closed the gate and hit the button to return to the ground floor.

Dan opened the door to the reception area of the Director's office and followed Sally inside. The room was large, with dark red carpet stretching from wall to wall. It was capable of holding two dozen comfortably; a long couch sat against one wall, with four high back chairs circled around a low table closer to the door. A desk sat against the far wall, with a young brunette sitting behind it. Leaning over the desk talking to the woman was a man in his mid-twenties, wearing a dark pinstripe suit.

Dan hung his coat on the rack next to Sally's. Without speaking, he touched her on the arm and pointed at the man chatting up the secretary. Sally smiled and moved over to the couch. Dan quietly approached the man from behind.

Neither the man in the pinstripe suit nor the woman behind the desk noticed Dan as he neared the desk. The man had dark, curly hair, while the woman's brunette locks were done up in a tight bun. She wore a light blue dress that highlighted her curves, even though all that Dan could see of her was above the waist. Whatever the man was saying to her had her completely enthralled.

Dan stood about two feet behind the man and crossed his arms.

"Always on the alert, eh, Kendal? Except when there's a beautiful woman to talk to?"

The man wheeled around as if reaching for the gun in his shoulder holster. Dan dropped his elbows to his sides, his hands outward, as if he were ready to wrestle. A look of recognition dawned on the other man's face.

"Ha! Fowler, you old hoot! Don't you know not to sneak up on a seasoned agent, especially one as legendary as Larry Kendal?"

Dan laughed and put his hands on his hips. "Seasoned? You?"

Larry returned the laugh and extended his hand to his friend. Dan stepped closer and shook the outstretched hand firmly. Larry's blue eyes beamed as he smiled, his young face belying his age; small lines could be seen at the corners of his eyes.

"Good to see you, Larry," said Dan as he clapped the other man on the shoulder with his free hand.

"You too, Dan." He gestured over his shoulder with his thumb. "I was just telling Juliette her about our adventure in Borneo last year."

Dan looked around his friend at the young woman behind the desk. She smiled widely and avoided Dan's eyes.

"I'm sure he told you the true account," remarked Dan, as he looked sideways at his friend. "Larry Kendal has never been known to stretch the truth regarding his exploits for the Bureau."

Juliette met Dan's gaze. "It seemed completely believable to me, Mr. Fowler," she replied, still smiling.

Sally appeared at Dan's left shoulder. "Half of what these boys tell you isn't true, my dear, and the other half they only wished had happened."

Dan and Larry both laughed at this as Sally approached the Director's office door.

"Come along, boys," said Sally. "We don't want to keep the Chief waiting."

The Chief Director of the FBI leaned forward in his high-backed office chair, regarding the three people seated before his desk. His black hair showed a touch of gray around the temples. He was clean-shaven, and his heavy eyebrows moved slightly as he shifted his steady brown eyes between those seated opposite of him. A morning newspaper next to his right hand declared the headline "Nuremberg Laws Begin to Take Hold in Germany." Dan, Sally, and Larry sat silently, waiting for the Chief to finish the thought he'd just started. A half-smoked cigar lay smoldering in the ashtray next to the Chief's left hand.

"Like I said," continued the Chief, "this new German attaché has some serious connections. His father has noble blood. Can trace it all the way back to Conrad the Third."

"Wow, that's nearly eight hundred years!" remarked Larry while playing with the lapel of his jacket.

"And he doesn't feel bad about reminding you about it," added the Chief.

"What did you say his name was?" asked Dan.

"Heinrich Berengar," answered the Chief.

"And only twenty-five years old," Sally interjected. "Awfully young for a diplomatic attaché."

"Like I said," stated the Chief, "his father is of noble blood and has lots of influence. He was a close friend of Wilhelm II, but I'm told that he has given, at least on the surface, support for Hitler's new government."

"What's he doing in D.C.?" Larry asked, taking a silver cigarette case out of his suit pocket.

"His father is sponsoring an exhibit at the National Gallery that features ancient German artifacts," said the Chief. "Things from the Middle Ages and whatnot. Heinrich will be meeting with members of the Cabinet and giving them a private tour. He has requested a security detail, but heaven knows why – he has the biggest bodyguard you've ever seen."

"How big?" asked Dan, glancing sideways at Sally. She smiled slightly, keeping her eyes on the Chief.

"The guy could throw a Panzer a quarter mile," the Chief remarked. "His name is Otto. He doesn't say much. You'll like him, Kendal." The Chief smiled and picked up his cigar. He stuck it in his mouth and lit it before continuing.

"You'll meet Heinrich at the brownstone he's rented at eight o'clock tomorrow morning. He'll have the rest of the details for you then."

Dan, Sally, and Larry slid their chairs back and stood up. The Chief leaned back in his chair and puffed on his cigar. Sally and Larry made for the door first. Dan lingered behind.

"Something on your mind, Fowler?" asked the Chief.

Dan pondered for a second, then answered.

"You feel comfortable with Germans in the capital, Chief, given what's been going on over there the past few years?"

"I'm comfortable with your ability to do your job, Fowler." The Chief turned to Sally and Larry, still standing by the door.

"I'm comfortable with all of your abilities. Should things go south, I know you all can handle yourselves."

Larry gave a slight nod. "You can count on that, Chief."

The Chief took his cigar out of his mouth and leaned forward.

"Oh, and Fowler," he said with a smile. "I expect you to play nice."

Dan returned the smile and then followed Sally and Larry out of the office.

The next morning, Dan, Sally, and Larry pulled up in front of the address that Juliette had given them. Larry drove, completely at home behind the wheel of the large automobile in which they all sat, with Dan in the front passenger seat and Sally in the back. The car was a sleek black color, and had been outfitted with special plates that ran from front to back. The car didn't appear bulky, but the special armor made it nearly indestructible. The additional buttons on the dashboard could activate the surprises it had hiding under its armor, should there be any attempt to attack or steal it.

Larry drummed on the steering wheel and looked at the tall brownstone in front of which they had parked.

"Want to just go up and ring the doorbell?" he asked.

"Nah," replied Dan. "You and Sally stay here. I'm going to have a look around before we go in."

Dan opened the car door and stepped out onto the sidewalk. The sun was shining, but the air was still cold, and Dan pulled his long coat around himself before approaching the gate leading to the front sidewalk. He opened the gate and stepped off the sidewalk, heading to his right across the frozen grass. He walked down the side of the house, glancing up at the three stories above. There were multiple windows on each floor, all with the curtains closed.

Dan reached the back of the house and turned into a small yard. The grass stretched from a set of back stairs to a tall wooden fence approximately twenty feet away. He walked to the fence and put his hands on top of the slats. Pulling himself up on his tiptoes, he surveyed the cluster of trees that bordered the property. He turned his head left and right, but saw nothing but dense trees and undergrowth. Through a slight clearing, he could see the back of another brownstone.

"Can I help you with something, Herr Fowler?" came a deep, thick German voice from behind him.

Dan wheeled around and reached instinctively for his gun in his shoulder holster, stopping just in time as he saw who had spoken. Before him was the largest man he'd ever set eyes on. The man stood nearly seven feet tall, with broad shoulders and thick legs. He wore a fine black suit that had to have been custom-made by a very skilled tailor. His short, cropped hair was bright blonde, and his eyes were a blue-white color. How he had snuck up on Dan without making a sound was beyond the experienced agent's comprehension.

Dan eased his hands to his sides and stood up straight, making sure not to move too quickly.

"You must be Otto," he said.

"Yes," replied the gargantuan man.

"I was just getting a sense of the property," Dan continued, keeping his eyes locked on the other man's, even though he wanted to survey him up and down, just to see again how large he really was.

Otto turned his hips and gestured towards the back of the brownstone.

"If you'll follow me, Herr Fowler, your friends are already inside."

"Sure thing," Dan nodded and followed Otto to the back door.

Dan walked into a large sitting room on the first floor of the brownstone. Larry and Sally were seated in two high-backed chairs, facing a slender, upright man in a third chair. A fourth seat waited for him.

The man stood as Dan approached his chair. Otto came in behind and closed the door. There was large desk set against the far wall to Dan's right, and built-in bookshelves lined the wall in front of him. Various pieces of art adorned the walls, and to his left stood floor-length windows with blue curtains that had been drawn back to let in the morning sunlight. A fireplace behind the four chairs held three logs that were crackling with a warm glow.

"Greetings, Herr Fowler," said the man, his German accent only slightly tingeing his English. "I am Heinrich Berengar. Thank you for coming." He extended his hand.

Dan gave a slight nod and shook the proffered hand. Heinrich had a thin, gangly appearance, but he wore an impeccable suit of dark blue that had clearly been made for him, along with a matching tie. His silk pocket square peeked out from his breast pocket, and a silver wristwatch glinted as it caught the light. He had a pale complexion, and his short dark hair was neatly combed back. He wore round glasses that sat straight on his long nose. Dan held the handshake for a few seconds as he surveyed the other man, not moving his eyes too much.

"Please, sit," said Heinrich, gesturing to the empty chair. He sat down in his own chair and placed his hands on the armrests, sitting as upright as possible.

Dan sat down and gave a quick glance in Sally's direction. She gave a slight smile, looking at Heinrich the entire time. Larry was sitting back in his chair patiently, watching their host with interest.

"I would like to thank you all for coming," Heinrich began. "As you know, this trip is very important to my father, as it is to me. The National Gallery exhibit will have on display some of the rarest and most valuable antiquities from the time of my ancestor, Conrad the Third."

"We understand the importance of the exhibit," said Dan as he leaned forward slightly in his chair. Otto had moved to stand directly behind Heinrich's chair, and Dan had a hard time not moving his eyes to the large man. Focusing again, he continued. "What's not so clear is what role you would like us to play."

Heinrich smiled before he responded.

"I'm sure you're wondering why a German diplomatic attaché such as myself would want the help of the FBI in this matter. To be frank, Herr Fowler, my father and I have heard of your exploits, and when it comes to the exhibit's security, there's no one we'd rather have than you."

Dan sat back in his chair and folded his hands in his lap.

"Well, that's nice of you to say, but the FBI doesn't offer private security to just anyone, you know."

Heinrich smiled again, keeping his gaze on Dan.

"The Secretary of State assured my father that we would be granted whatever we needed during our stay, and my father is adamant that we have nothing but the best when it comes to this exhibit."

Dan half-smiled and sat more upright in his chair.

"Very well," he said. "But what about Larry and Sally? If I'm planning the security detail, what roles will they play?"

"Herr Kendal will be your second in command," Heinrich replied. "He will be in charge of securing the perimeter of the main exhibit gallery. As for Fraulein Vane, she will be in charge of security clearances before and the identification checks during both the private viewing for the President and the Cabinet, and the opening gala."

Dan nodded and looked up at Otto, who was still standing with his arms crossed behind Heinrich's chair. The giant man's eyes were locked on Dan.

"And what about Otto here? Where will he be?"

"He'll be where he always is," Heinrich answered. "Taking care of my personal security at all times."

"Well, it sounds like you've thought of everything," Larry chimed in.

Heinrich turned to regard Larry. "Of course we have, Herr Kendal. We Germans are very thorough when it comes to matters such as these."

Larry gave a half smile. "When do we start?" he asked.

"Tomorrow," Heinrich answered. "I will send instructions on where and when to meet. The Cabinet viewing is at six o'clock tomorrow evening, and the opening gala begins precisely at eight."

Heinrich stood from his chair and smoothed the creases from his suit jacket. Dan, Sally, and Larry followed his lead and stood from their seats. Otto moved to open the parlor door.

"I thank you all again for coming," said Heinrich, "and for your willingness to help in this matter. I eagerly await our next meeting. Otto will see you out."

With that, he stepped quickly to the door and disappeared up the stairs to the second floor. Otto held the door open and waited for the three agents to exit.

Larry led the way to the front door, with Dan and Sally right behind. Dan gave Otto a curt nod as he passed the giant man. Otto followed Dan with his eyes. Once the front door was open, Dan sidled down the steps with Sally, onto the sidewalk, and through the front gate. After hearing the front door close behind them, Dan leaned over to Sally and whispered.

"That seem as strange to you as it did to me?"

Sally looked up and down the sidewalk before gripping the door handle of the car. She gave Dan a wry smile.

"Only slightly."

The next morning, Dan Fowler sat on the couch in his apartment, cleaning his .357 blue steel revolver. It was nearly seven o'clock, and he was wearing socks, his black suit pants, and a white undershirt. His shoulder holster sat on the coffee table in front of him, with an old newspaper opened up next to it so that oil wouldn't get everywhere as he cleaned his gun.

Putting the parts back together, Dan cocked the hammer back and looked down the length of the gun. The steel felt right in his hand, and he extended his arm outwards and then back in, feeling the weight of the revolver. He loaded six shells into it and laid it on the table next to the holster.

The phone on the end table next to the couch gave a shrill ring. Wiping his hands on a rag next to him, he reached over, picked up the receiver, and held it to his ear.

"'Ello," he stated.

"Dan, it's Larry," came the voice from the other end of the line. "I'm at the office. Berengar just called. We're meeting him at eight o'clock at the east entrance of the National Gallery."

"And Sally?" Dan asked.

"Already called her. She said she'd take a cab and meet us there. I'll be there to get you in fifteen."

"Sounds good. See yah then, pal."

Fifteen minutes later, Dan stood on the sidewalk in front of his apartment building, wearing his long coat. The loaded revolver sat snugly in its shoulder holster, six extra bullets stuck in the small bandolier above the gun. Dan stuck his hands in his pockets. He'd donned a black fedora that Sally had given him as a gift last Christmas.

Larry pulled up to the curb in his long black car. Dan got in the passenger side and pulled the door shut as Larry started down the street.

"Cold enough for yah, Dan?" Larry asked as Dan settled into his seat.

"Nah," Dan replied, "We had colder winters back where I grew up."

"Oh, you Midwestern boys are a hearty stock," Larry laughed as they stopped at a red light. "Makes me glad you're working for the Bureau and not slinging hay bales in some cow town."

"Best twenty five cents a day I ever made," Dan chuckled.

"I bet our new friend Otto could throw some hay bales," said Larry as he turned a corner and headed west on Constitution Avenue.

"Ooh boy, I bet he could. How do you think the Germans grow 'em so

Larry pulled up to the curb...

big?" asked Dan.

"I dunno, pal," Larry replied. "But I would not want to be on the wrong side of him. Those eyes are enough to scare the ghost out of a man."

"And what about his employer?" Dan continued.

"Herr Berengar seems awfully sure of himself," answered Larry. "He seemed pleasant enough, but there was something behind those eyes."

"I agree," said Dan. "Something seemed a bit off, but I can't quite put my finger on it. It's been needling at me since we met him."

"Well, maybe we'll get some answers during our private tour of his exhibit."

"Maybe," Dan replied. "We'll find out soon enough."

After leaving the car parked at the curb on the east side of the National Gallery, Dan and Larry made their way into the building and down a hallway that led to a small landing with two doors on either side of it. Illuminated by sconces, a set of stairs continued down towards the main part of the building. Otto stood next to the door on the right, his hulking frame filling the small niche where the wall met a pillar of marble.

"Good morning, Otto," said Dan, taking off his hat and giving the large man a small nod.

"Good morning, Herr Fowler, Herr Kendal," Otto replied to the two men as they approached. "Herr Berengar is inside. Fraulein Vane is waiting as well."

"Well, let's not stand around chatting about the weather," said Larry, smiling from ear to ear.

Otto opened the door and gestured for the two men to enter. Dan and Larry passed the threshold and the large German pulled the door shut behind them before returning to his post. For a moment, Dan thought he heard the door lock when it closed. Turning his head back down the hallway, he followed Larry to a set of double doors.

Larry opened the doors to find Heinrich and Sally sitting in two chairs around a small table. Sally had her back to the door and turned as her friends entered.

"Good morning, boys," she smiled as she stood. Heinrich stood as well and extended his hand as Dan and Larry joined them. Larry shook first as Dan gave Sally a warm smile. After greeting Heinrich as well, he sat down in an empty chair.

"I'm very glad you're all here," Heinrich started. "I'm very excited to begin."

On the table in front of him sat a map of the National Gallery, its floors laid out in a grid, showing each hallway, stairwell, and exhibit space. Dan put his coat and hat on the table next to the map and scanned it quickly, trying to memorize the layout in his head. The building's basement stood out to him in particular. The map of the lowest level showed a labyrinthine tangle of corridors, some wide, some narrow, and a number of rooms, some large, some small. Whoever had designed the building didn't skip any steps in laying out the basement.

A person could get lost down there for days, Dan thought to himself.

Heinrich leaned forward in his chair and pointed to the main gallery space on the first floor.

"My father's exhibit is here, in the main gallery. It spans the entire length of the hall, and glass cases have been arranged to protect the artifacts. You, Herr Fowler, will be in charge of ensuring that no one enters or exits but by the main door, here." Heinrich pointed to a large set of double doors that led from the main entrance of the building to the gallery.

"Fraulein Vane will be checking identification clearances here," Berengar continued, "just outside the main door. Herr Kendal will be walking the perimeter, making sure that no one strays too far from the exhibit."

Dan surveyed the map, making mental notes of all the doors, windows, and other points of interest. After a minute, he leaned back in his chair.

"Seems simple enough. Which Cabinet members will be in attendance for the private viewing, and how many are you expecting for the gala opening?"

"The Secretary of State has assured my father that the entire Cabinet will be present. The President and the First Lady will arrive shortly after the Cabinet, I am told. Approximately fifty guests, most of them various dignitaries, ambassadors, and government officials have been invited to the gala. The Secret Service will of course provide the President's personal detail."

"Is it possible for us to see the exhibit before the private viewing?" Larry asked.

"Of course, Herr Kendal," Heinrich replied, rising from his chair. "If you will but follow me."

After leading them through a side door from the sitting room, Heinrich guided them down a hallway that led to a curving set of stairs. At the bottom, he unlocked a single door that opened into the north side of the main gallery. Dan followed Larry and Sally through as Heinrich held the door for them.

"Take a moment to peruse, please," said Heinrich. "I want you to have a complete sense of the room."

Glass cases of varying heights and widths filled the gallery. Behind each one stood a variety of axes and swords, helmets and shields. Three ornate chandeliers hung from the ceiling, bouncing their light off the glass throughout the room. Curved sconces lined the walls between several doors, and the only daylight was coming from the main door across from where they stood.

In one case in the center of the room was a tall, ornate mask. Made of wood, it had a human-like nose, and the eyes were mere slits topped with red glyphs. The mouth was turned down and the ears protruded into points that almost resembled horns. The mask had once been painted blue or green, and from top to bottom had to measure nearly two feet. It sat on a glass shelf in the case, which itself was taller than an average man. Two identical cases, both empty, stood on either side of it.

Walking to the center case, Dan stopped to observe the mask, studying its features. Sally and Larry walked up behind him and studied it as well. From behind the glass case, the distorted shape of Heinrich could be seen, his hands behind his back. A smile came to his face as he began to speak.

"The legends say that my ancestor Conrad the Third acquired that mask following the Second Battle of Dorylaeum in 1147. The Turkish enemy led by Mesud the First had many soldiers, and among them were warriors who wore these masks. According to my father's research, they were meant to invoke some form of deity and give them power over their enemies. After the Turks routed Conrad's army, these warriors pursued the Germans for many miles. Conrad's men thought they had finally given up, but two nights after the battle, a single warrior crept into the German camp, in an attempt to assassinate the King. Unfortunately, the alarm was raised and the warrior was slain before he could reach Conrad's tent. The King's men claimed that when the man was killed, his body turned to dust and the mask fell to the earth as if it weighed a hundred pounds. No one dared touch it, until the King approached, picked it up, and took it back to his tent."

Dan, Sally, and Larry looked at each other as Heinrich finished his tale.

"That's quite a story there, Herr Berengar," Larry said after a moment.

"And this is quite a mask," Dan added.

"That face and that story are going to give me nightmares for weeks," Sally commented, moving away from the case and towards the main doors.

Heinrich stepped around the case to gaze at the mask with Dan and Larry.

"This piece is the crowning artifact of my father's collection. It is imperative that it remain safely behind the glass, and that no one gets too close to it." He looked out of the corner of his eye at Dan and Larry. "It has been said that some men become entranced by staring at it too long."

Dan shook his head and turned towards Heinrich. Nudging Larry with his elbow, he brought his friend's attention back to the matters at hand.

"Very interesting tale, to be sure," Dan said, taking in the rest of the room, then gesturing to the two empty cases next to the one that held the mask. "What are these two cases for?" he asked.

"Those are for two very special exhibits," replied Heinrich. "Traditional garb that was believed to be worn by Mesud's fabled warriors."

"Where are the mannequins?" Larry inquired.

"They are soon to arrive," said Heinrich as he stepped around the nearest case, a slight smile on his face.

"I'm going to have a look around and see which doors need to be secured," Dan continued.

"Very well," Heinrich replied, giving a slight nod. "I shall see if Fraulein Vane has found everything to her satisfaction."

Dan walked to the far side of the room, checking the doors along the west wall of the gallery. Larry walked the opposite wall, doing the same. Each door was locked and made of heavy oak. Dan checked one particularly heavy door that would take a man of great strength to break down or wrench open by force.

"I bet Otto could manage it," Dan muttered under his breath.

When he and Larry met at the door by which they'd entered the room, they stopped and turned back towards the exhibit. They stood perhaps fifty feet from the center display cases and the ancient Turkish mask.

"Seems simple enough, Danny boy," said Larry, putting his hands in his pockets and surveying the room.

"Agreed," Dan replied, copying his friend's stance. "I'm still not sold on why the Chief thought we needed to take on this assignment. I suppose he had some pressure from the top."

"Most likely," Larry chuckled. "After all, we wouldn't want anything to happen to our new friend Heinrich and his daddy's fancy mask."

Before Larry could finish his thought, the lights in the main gallery went out and the room was bathed in total darkness. A woman's scream came from the doors near the main entrance, followed by the sound of breaking glass. Dan and Larry pulled their guns, but didn't bring them to bear on anything as their eyes adjusted to the sudden loss of light.

"Sally?" Dan yelled, taking a step forward. Before he could take another, the lights came back on.

"Dan, look!" Larry yelled, pointing to the middle of the room. There, where the case holding the ancient mask had stood, the display was knocked over and glass shards covered the floor. The mask was nowhere to be seen.

Dan's eyes moved from the broken case to the doors that led to the main entrance. They had been thrown open with such force that one on the left was hanging off of its hinges. Heinrich and Sally were nowhere in sight. A massive form filled the entryway, its face concealed by a wooden mask.

"Oh my god," Dan started, blinking at the scene in front of him. "What in the hell is that?"

Dan and Larry stood in the main exhibit hall of the National Gallery, staring at the hulking form of a man that filled the main entrance. They pointed their guns at the figure and slowly stepped forward. On the massive man's face sat a mask that was very similar to the one that had been on display behind the case that now sat broken in the middle of the hall. The only difference in the two was that the one on this man's face was much larger. The man wore a large robe of green and blue vertical stripes, with a sash of dark red around his middle. He seemed to be staring at the floor.

"Otto?" Dan began, inching his way forward. "Otto, what is going on?"

"Big fella doesn't seem himself," Larry said as he mirrored Dan's movements, his right index finger on the trigger of his .38, his left hand holding the butt of the gun. The giant in front of them did not move or give any indication that he heard them.

"Otto," Dan continued, moving towards the display cases in the middle. "Where is Sally?"

The large man slowly raised his head. When they saw the eyes of the mask, Dan and Larry both froze where they stood.

"Dan? What is happening?" Larry said through clenched teeth. "I can't move!"

"Me neither," Dan replied, trying to will his legs to keep walking.

Larry slowly moved his eyes to the left. In his peripheral vision, he saw one of the doors on the perimeter of the room open. As it did, another figure wearing a robe and a mask stepped into the hall.

"Dan, we've got company."

Dan moved his eyes to his right. The door closest to him had also opened, and a figure in a robe and a mask now stood there, gazing at him.

"We sure do."

As they stood frozen in place, both men could hear other doors opening and closing. Before long, the entire perimeter of the main exhibit hall was lined with masked figures wearing green and blue robes with dark red sashes.

Turning his eyes back towards the main entrance, Dan saw an elderly man step around Otto's large form and walk towards them. His hair was long and white and he wore the same attire as those standing around the room. Under his arm, he carried another mask. He smiled as he approached the two men.

"Greetings, Herr Fowler, Herr Kendal." He spoke with a thick German accent. "My name is Gustav Wilhelm Berengar. Thank you so very much for agreeing to be a part of my exhibit."

The older man took the mask from under his arm and held it out for them to see. "This mask is the original that my ancestor took from the Turkish warrior who had snuck into the German camp. What you are experiencing now is the powerful force that the warrior would exert on his enemies to stop them where they stood. The warrior would only free his enemy for a moment before he struck, just enough time to return hope to the man's heart. Many would think they had overcome the mask's power, only to be cut down moments later by the warrior's blade."

Gustav smiled as he put the mask over his face. "I'm sure you feel, Herr Fowler, that you are powerful enough to break free. After all, with the things you've accomplished in your life, why not?"

Even though the mask obscured the old man's features, Dan could sense the smile.

"Not really, no," Dan replied. "But I don't need to move my whole body. Just my trigger finger."

With Gustav standing so close, Dan had a clear shot at Otto, who was still taking up the doorway of the main entrance. With every ounce of his will, he squeezed the trigger of his revolver. The bullet sped through the space where the glass case had stood and connected with the wooden mask on the hulking man's face. Splinters and blood went flying.

Gustav screamed from behind his mask and wheeled around as Otto went crashing to the floor. The large man sent chunks of tile everywhere. The other figures around the room screamed as well and brandished daggers that had been hidden in their sashes.

"Dan, we're free!" Larry yelled as he moved his left leg. Dan moved to grab Gustav, but with a flash of smoke and light, the old man seemed to disappear into the floor. Dan turned to engage with the onrushing attackers. He fired a round that took the first man through the heart. Before he could cock the hammer back again, another robed figure was on top of him, stabbing at him from above. Dan blocked the attack with his left arm and smashed the butt of his gun into the man's solar plexus. A rush of air came through the mask as the man fell to the floor.

Larry fired a shot that hit a masked assailant square in the face. Blood sprayed the attacker behind him, momentarily blinding him. Larry stepped to the side as his first attacker fell, then shot the second through the heart. More robed figures surrounded him, wielding their daggers, but not moving any closer.

Dan grappled with another robed figure as the man grabbed his right wrist. Turning his hips, Dan put his left arm under the man's right shoulder and tossed him to the floor. He kicked the attacker square in the face, splitting the wooden mask in two.

Dan turned to regard the rest of his assailants, who were now keeping their distance. Dan leveled his gun at the nearest one.

"Now fellas," he said, panting slightly. "If you'll just give us Miss Vane, we'll be on our way."

The robed figure closest to Dan began to make a sound that could have been a laugh. His body didn't move, but the sound was clearly coming from his mask.

"Very well, Herr Fowler," the figure spoke. It was the voice of Gustav Berengar. "Come and find her!"

The lights in the main hall went out again. When they came back on, only the bodies of the dead remained. The rest had vanished, even the fallen body of Otto near the main doors.

"Find her where?" Larry asked, his eyes darting around the room.

Dan put his revolver back in his holster.

"The basement."

Dan and Larry made their way back to the room where they'd met Heinrich earlier that morning. Dan had hoped that the map of the building was still there, but when they reached the parlor, the table was bare and the room was empty.

"What now?" Larry asked, his gun still in his hand.

"We start opening doors," Dan replied.

"Don't you think we ought to let the Chief know what's going on?" Larry continued.

Dan looked at his watch. "It's nearly eight-thirty, he's likely just now getting to the office. We need to find Sally and see what Heinrich and Gustav have planned. There's a reason they brought us here this morning, and I don't think it's anything good."

Larry sighed and put his gun into his shoulder holster. "Alright, but if we haven't found her in the next thirty minutes, I'm finding a phone and ringing the Chief."

The two agents left the parlor and made their way back to the hallway where Otto had greeted them. Another large door lined the wall opposite of where they were standing.

"At least the car's still there," Larry remarked, pointing outside to where he'd parked his vehicle.

Dan opened the door on the other side of the hallway. Behind it, a large staircase led down into the lower levels of the building. There was one light bulb hanging above the top landing, but below there was nothing but darkness.

"This way, Larry," Dan said as he stepped into the stairwell.

Larry followed behind as Dan descended the stairs. Dan reached the first landing and removed his gun from his shoulder holster. He opened the chamber, popped out the two empty shells and inserted two new bullets. When he snapped the chamber shut, the sound echoed off the concrete walls.

Larry brandished his gun as well. He stayed a stair or two behind Dan, checking behind them every few steps. Dan continued downwards, his eyes adjusting to the lack of light the further he went. After two flights, they reached a door.

Dan put his hand on the knob and slowly turned it. The door was unlocked and creaked as he opened it. Stepping through, Dan scanned left and right down the hallway. There was no light, but as his eyes adjusted, he could see that it stretched as far as he could see in either direction, with doors and other corridors joining it in various places.

His instincts told him to go left, so he did. Larry stepped in behind him, keeping his eyes to the left, covering Dan's back. When Dan reached the first connecting hallway, he slowly pressed himself against the wall. After a count of three, he turned the corner, pointing his gun straight ahead. All he could see was more hallway bathed in darkness and what seemed to be another door at the end, nearly forty feet from where he stood.

"It really is a maze down here," Larry whispered as he stood against the wall next to Dan.

"Sally could be anywhere," Dan replied in his own hushed tone. "You didn't happen to bring a flashlight, did you?"

"Pretty sure it's in my other pants," Larry smiled, the flash of his teeth bright in the dim corridor. Dan allowed himself a half smirk as he turned to continue down the main hallway.

After another twenty feet, they came to another door. It was solid oak, and had an ornate knob with a skeleton key lock. Dan moved to the far side of the door while Larry turned the knob. The door stuck for a moment, then swung inward when Larry gave it a firm push.

Inside was a chair with ropes hanging from the back of it. Dan stepped into the room quietly, his gun at eye level. Stopping, he sniffed the air. He held up his hand for Larry to stop.

"You smell that?" Dan asked.

Larry stopped and sniffed the air. "Smells like perfume."

"Exactly," Dan continued. "Sally's perfume. She was in here, just a few minutes ago." Usually Sally's scent made his heart rate pick up, but now his heart was beating faster for another reason.

Larry moved to the corner and knelt where a gas lantern sat, its flame turned down low. A voice filled the room. "You're running out of time, gentleman." It was Gustav, and it sounded like he was standing right next to them.

Dan wheeled around and pointed his gun at the open door. "I'm also running out of patience!" he shouted at the disembodied voice. The only response was faint laughter that seemed to come from the hallway.

Stepping back into the hall, Dan surveyed both directions. The laugh had sounded like it had come from further into the bowels of the building. As Dan moved to follow it, the door behind him slammed shut, Larry still in the room.

"Larry!" Dan grabbed the knob, but it wouldn't budge. From the other side, he could hear Larry shouting and pounding on the door.

"Dan! Dan! Help me!"

Dan threw his shoulder against the door. When it didn't budge, he tried to force it open again. Throwing himself against it a third time, he heard Larry scream again. On the fourth try, the door sprang open, almost spilling him onto the floor.

Inside, the gas lantern was still burning low. There was no sign of Larry, save for his gun that sat on the floor near the empty chair. Dan picked it up and put it into his shoulder holster, his gun still in his hand.

Dan surveyed the room for any other entrance, any crack in the wall, floor, or ceiling. He moved to the wall behind the chair and began pressing it with his hand. The stone was cold to the touch at first, but as he walked toward the middle, he felt a draft move past his fingers. Studying it with his hand, since it was too dark for his eyes to make out any fissure, he found where the draft was coming from.

Pushing harder, he felt one of the stones move. It slid to the left, revealing a hidden handle set into the wall. It felt like iron in his hand, and grasping it, he turned it clockwise. He felt something click, and the wall in front of him swung inwards on hidden hinges.

Before him stretched another hallway, but this one was not dark. Every ten feet or so, iron sconces held burning torches. Dan could see more halls branching off of the corridor and more doors as far as he could see. At the end of the hall sat another large door.

Has to be at least a hundred yards away, Dan thought to himself.

He took a few wary steps into the hallway, keeping his gun at the ready. As he passed the first torch, he turned to look behind him. The stone door still sat open, and he could see the empty room with the empty chair.

Turning back around, his field of vision was completely blocked. Moving his eyes up, he took in the hulking form of Otto standing in front of him.

Otto still wore the green and blue robe with the red sash, but his face was free of the mask. On his forehead was a large red welt where Dan's bullet had seemingly grazed him.

Dan moved to bring his gun to bear on the gargantuan man, but the brute moved too quickly. With his left hand, Otto grabbed Dan's right wrist. With his right, the massive bodyguard swung a fist hard into Dan's jaw. Dan's head swam, and before falling unconscious, he saw the gleaming white of Otto's teeth and his bright blue eyes in the light of the torches burning all around him.

Dan slowly opened his eyes. His vision was blurred and his head felt like it had a thousand bees buzzing around inside of it. He blinked a few times, letting his eyes clear. To his left, he saw Larry tied to a chair, unconscious. To his right was Sally in the same state. When he made to move, Dan realized he was also tied to a chair. They were in a larger room than the one with the lantern and the single chair. This one had the same torches and the same iron sconces as the hallway where Otto had knocked him out. There was a long table lining the far wall, next to the only door that Dan could see. From where he sat, it appeared to be the other side of the same door he'd spotted at the end of the long hallway, before Otto had shown up.

Two figures stood in front of him, dressed in blue and green robes. Moving his eyes to their faces, Dan saw Heinrich and Gustav Berengar smiling down at him.

"Welcome, Herr Fowler," said Heinrich. He held his wooden mask under his arm. Behind him in the corner stood the hulking form of Otto. "I apologize for what Otto had to do to you, but my father and I knew you would never come along willingly."

Dan moved his jaw from side to side, feeling the effects of the punch Otto had given him. "That was quite a punch, I'll give him that." Dan moved his eyes to the large man. "He moves quick for such a large fella, but if he ever tries it again, there will be a different result." Otto smiled from his spot in the corner.

Gustav laughed and stepped forward. "Ah, such American resilience. I love how dedicated you all are to the idea that no one can beat you twice." The old man bent down to look Dan square in the eyes. "But that's just it, Herr Fowler, you are already beaten. In a few hours' time, the Cabinet and the President will arrive, and you will help us persuade them to join our cause. You will help usher in a new era – an era of power and stability, where all men's hearts are laid bare for the rightful king to judge."

"Like hell I will," Dan spat in response.

"Herr Fowler, you are already beaten."

Gustav smiled and stood up. "You have no choice in the matter. You've already felt the power of the mask, and soon you'll be totally under its control. There is no hope of escape."

"You seem to forget that I'm a federal agent," Dan replied, "and that if I don't check in at least once today, my chief will send all the agents he has to this building."

Gustav glanced at his son and his smile grew wider. Heinrich took his mask from under his arm and put it over his face. Dan tried not to meet his gaze, but his own eyes seemed to disobey him.

"The power of the mask is not something that can be overcome," said Heinrich from behind his wooden visage. "It has more secrets than you know."

"Is that supposed to scare me?" asked Dan.

"You know very well that it should," Heinrich replied, but not in his own voice. Instead, the voice that came from the mask was Dan's own. Everything, from the intonation to the cadence, was perfect. Dan's eyes grew wide and his mouth fell open.

"How…how the hell…"

Gustav laughed and folded his arms across his chest. "I assure you that your chief director will hear from you, Herr Fowler. You will check in with him soon to let him know that things are going perfectly."

The older man walked over to the table and picked up his mask. Putting it on, he turned back to Dan.

"Now, we have much to prepare," came his voice from behind the mask. "When you wake again, you will be one step closer to helping us realize what we came here to do."

"And what might that be?" Dan asked as he felt his eyes grow heavy once again.

"All in good time, Herr Fowler," Gustav replied. "All in good time."

Dan tried to force his eyes to stay open, but they wouldn't obey. His head began to swim, and his mind became a jumble of thoughts and emotions. He saw Sally, Larry, and the Chief in the Bureau office, and then his father popped into his head. Dan was holding his father during his final moments, having been shot by gangsters in the street. He tried to focus on the memory, but the two glaring eyes of the wooden mask suddenly grew larger in his mind, and they were the last thing he remembered before his chin fell to his chest.

The Chief Director sat back in his desk chair to rest his eyes from the papers he had been studying for nearly an hour. New agent assignments had kept him busy since he'd arrived at the Bureau that morning, and he knew that he'd be at it for at least another hour.

He opened the ornate wooden box on the left-hand side of the desk and pulled out a fresh cigar. Opening his middle desk drawer, he retrieved his cigar cutter and a box of matches. After snipping the end of the cigar, he brushed the cut end into the wastebasket and pulled a match from the box. Striking it, he lit the cigar and looked down the end of his nose, watching the red glow of the tobacco leaf as it caught. Inhaling, he held it for a moment and then exhaled a plume of smoke.

Glancing at his watch, he realized it was nearly ten o'clock and he hadn't heard from Dan or Larry yet that morning. He'd never set a schedule for the Berengar detail, but it was normal for Dan to call him at least once during the first day on assignment in the capital.

Just then, the phone on his desk began to ring. He held the cigar in his mouth as he reached for the receiver.

"Hello?" he said as he put the phone to his ear.

"Morning, Chief," came the voice of Dan Fowler from the other end of the line.

"Dan! I was just thinking about you. How's everything over at the gallery?"

"Fine, just fine," Dan replied. "Larry and I are just finalizing the security details for the gala tonight."

"Good, good," the Chief answered. "I can't tell you how much the Secretary of State insisted that you be on this detail. I know it's not the most exciting, but the Berengars were adamant, from what it sounds like."

"I understand, Chief. I'm happy to help. It's quite an interesting exhibit, if nothing else."

"Oh yeah?" asked the Chief. "I'm glad you're expanding your historical knowledge, Dan. Anything of particular interest?"

"A few items. There are some old weapons that I'm sure my dad would've loved to see."

The Chief gave a sideways look at the receiver in his hand. It wasn't like Dan to mention his father so nonchalantly.

"Yeah…yeah, Dan," he continued after a moment. "I'm sure he would have. Well, I'll let you get back to it. Let me know if anything of significance comes up."

"Will do, Chief," Dan replied. "Talk to you later."

The Chief hung up the phone and leaned back in his chair once more. He puffed a few times on his cigar, then ashed it in the tray on his desk. His mind went to Dan's father, who had been a sheriff in a Midwestern town. Dan rarely talked about him, usually only during serious conversations, and then he'd mostly share nuggets of wisdom his father had imparted on him. The conversation he'd just had with Dan made him feel that something wasn't quite right.

Picking up the phone again, he hit the red button in the lower left-hand corner.

"Juliette?" he said after a moment.

"Yes, Chief?" came his secretary's petite voice.

"Call for my car," he said while stamping out the cigar in the ashtray. "I'm going to pay the Secretary of State a visit and see what he call tell me about Gustav Berengar."

Dan Fowler opened his eyes to see the wooden visage of Gustav's mask staring back at him. After a moment, he realized that he was seeing the reflection of his own two eyes gazing back at him through the slits of the mask that covered his face. Beyond that, he could see the gallery exhibit hall, with the main doors directly in front of him. The two big wooden doors had been reset on their hinges and the tiles that Otto had damaged had seemingly been repaired.

He could feel the weight of the mask on his head, but when he tried to move his arms to take it off, they wouldn't obey. *They drugged me,* he thought as he tried to get his legs to move. They wouldn't obey either, but he could feel rough fabric touching his thighs and knees.

I'm wearing the mask and the robes, his mind continued. *They've dressed me in the damn robes and mask, and I'm standing in one of the glass display cases.*

His case was situated at a slight angle, and moving his eyes to the left, he saw two more cases with figures standing in them. In the middle was what appeared to be a shorter, more feminine figure, wearing the same mask and warrior garb that he was.

Sally.

To the left of that was another figure encased in glass. This figure was taller and more slender, the blue and green robe hanging loosely off its shoulders. The wooden mask on its face seemed to stare back at Dan.

Larry.

Dan tried to will his body to move once again, but to no avail. He couldn't even open his mouth to yell.

How long have I been out? He wondered. *How long have I been standing in this ruddy case?*

Just then, the main doors opened. In stepped Otto, once again dressed in his black suit. He held the door for Heinrich, who was followed by his father. Both wore matching dark blue suits, their pocket kerchiefs a crisp red to complement the fabric. Gustav was laughing as he spoke to a tall man in a black tuxedo who walked beside him. The man had short, white hair, and he scrutinized the gallery as he stepped inside.

"I assure you, Mister Secretary," said Gustav. "You've never seen an exhibit quite like this."

"I've studied German history quite extensively, Herr Berengar," the tall man replied as he adjusted his tuxedo jacket. "And I've never come across a story of Conrad the Third claiming a mask from one of Mesud's warriors."

That's the Secretary of State! Dan's mind screamed as the two men approached his case. Behind them came a group of men dressed in tuxedos.

"I assure you that the story is quite true," Gustav continued as they stepped up to the exhibit case. "See, here is one of them itself!" He gestured to Dan and the mask that covered his face. The Secretary of State took a pair of his glasses from his jacket pocket, positioned them on his nose, and peered through the glass.

The Cabinet viewing! Dan's thoughts raced. The mask must've done a good job of concealing the terror in his eyes, because the Secretary looked right at him and didn't seem to notice one bit. Dan scanned past the two men in front of him and recognized the Secretaries of Defense and the Treasury, as well as several other Cabinet members.

The Secretary of State leaned back from examining the mask that Dan wore and placed his glasses back in his pocket. Gustav smiled at the man and gave a quick glance in Dan's direction.

"Very realistic, Gustav, I have to admit. Even the mannequins you've used are quite impressive." He took in the cases where Sally and Larry stood. Regarding the middle case, the Secretary leaned in once again. The robes and mask hid all of Sally's feminine features, save for her height.

"Somewhat short for a Turkish warrior, wouldn't you say?"

"They were all shapes and sizes," Gustav replied. "The shorter men could be much deadlier in hand-to-hand combat, as they were harder to hit!"

The Secretary of State nodded his head and glanced at the case that held Larry. "I suppose you're right. Speaking of hand-to-hand combat, I thought Dan Fowler was handling the security detail for the Cabinet viewing and the opening gala."

"He is, most assuredly," said Heinrich as he joined the two men in front of the glass cases. "Herr Fowler and Herr Kendal are securing the perimeter of the building before the President arrives." Heinrich's eyes shifted to Dan for just a moment, then back to the Secretary. "I'm sure he'll be back shortly."

The rest of the Cabinet members were walking around the room, observing all of the weapons and artifacts on display throughout the gallery. Otto stood a few paces behind Heinrich as the younger man spoke with his father and the Secretary of State. Dan moved his eyes up to look at the gargantuan man, but Otto stared straight ahead, seemingly at nothing.

"Very well," said the Secretary, moving to walk around the glass cases.

"The Chief Director of the FBI paid me a visit today. He had some questions regarding you and this exhibit, and why you insisted that Dan Fowler handle the security." He stopped to look back at Otto, who was standing just behind Heinrich. "One would think that Otto here is all the security you'd need."

Gustav smiled and put a hand on the Secretary's shoulder. "Otto is definitely useful in certain situations, but we knew that for an exhibit in the capital, we needed an American mind such as Herr Fowler's. Additionally, we felt that the Cabinet and the President would feel more comfortable with one of your own in charge."

The Secretary gave a half smile as the men approached a case sitting in the corner of the gallery that held two spears and a ceremonial dagger. Dan followed them with his eyes the best he could. He wasn't able to hear them any longer, thanks to the thick glass surrounding him.

"I suppose you're right about that," the Secretary remarked, studying the weapons closely. "I assured the Chief that all was being handled, and that there was nothing to fear. In fact, I invited him to join us and see for himself." Pushing back his jacket sleeve, he checked the watch on his left wrist. "It's nearly six fifteen now, I'm sure he'll be here soon."

Gustav and Heinrich exchanged smiles. Heinrich took a step back and gave a slight bow. "If you'll excuse me," he said, "I'll go make sure that Herr Fowler knows that the Chief is soon to arrive.

Dan watched as Heinrich took Otto by the arm and they both walked towards the main entrance. The shorter man was whispering something to the larger one, but Heinrich's hushed tones coupled with the thickness of the glass made it impossible for Dan to hear. Studying Heinrich's lips, he could tell the man was speaking German. Dan had often been able to read lips, but trying to figure out what someone was whispering in another language was a different challenge altogether.

After a few seconds, Otto moved away and walked through the doors towards the main entrance. Heinrich walked up to the case where Dan stood and tilted his head up. The German smiled wide before he turned to his right and made for one of the doors lining the perimeter of the gallery.

Dan's eyes shifted back to the main doors. He could see lights illuminating the hallway that led to the front entrance, but a set of steps blocked his view of the entry doors.

Gustav and the Secretary of State had moved back into the center of the room, a few steps from the cases that held Dan and his friends captive. Raising his arms outward, the older German addressed the room.

"My esteemed friends," he began. "I want to thank you all for joining us this evening for the opening. I hope you're finding the exhibit to be both interesting and exhilarating."

The remaining Cabinet members came to stand in front of Gustav, their backs turned to the cases that held Dan, Sally, and Larry. Dan wished he could see if his friends were awake and aware of what was going on around them.

"Before the President arrives," Gustav continued, "I'd like to provide you with a special demonstration that honors the history of my family, as well as the history of the German people. If you would turn towards the three cases in the middle of the gallery."

Dan watched as the Cabinet members turned to regard the cases that, to their eyes, held three mannequins wearing wooden masks and long blue and green warrior robes with red sashes. Something out of the corner of his eye caught Dan's attention. The doors around the room were opening, and entering the gallery was the cadre of masked and robed warriors that he and Larry had encountered earlier in the day.

The Cabinet members pointed and whispered to each other. Some were even smiling, thinking that this was all part of an elaborate presentation. Behind them, Gustav had moved to close the main gallery door. Once it was closed, he quietly clicked the lock shut.

They're all going to die, Dan thought as he tried to count the number of assassins filling the room. *They're all going to die and there's not a damn thing I can do about it.*

Gustav returned to his position in the center of the room and held his arms out once more.

"As you've likely noticed, our guests are wearing the same masks and robes as the displays in the center of the room. I assure you that all these artifacts are very real, but only a select few hold the true power of Mesud's warriors."

One of the masked figures came forward to stand directly in front of Dan's case. Judging by the build of the man and the way he walked, Dan knew it had to be Heinrich.

"This man wears is the original mask that was taken by my ancestor, Conrad the Third, following the Second Battle of Dorylaeum in 1147. The mask's fabled powers are often referenced throughout history, and it is my pleasure that you should witness them firsthand this evening."

With that, Heinrich stepped forward and pointed his gaze at the Secretary of State. The Secretary smiled for a moment, but then his eyes grew wide and the smile faded from his lips.

"Gustav?" he asked through clenched teeth. "Gustav, what sort of trick is this?"

Other masked and robed figures stepped beside Heinrich and directed their masks at the remaining Cabinet members. One by one, the men began to stiffen, their eyes growing wide. Unable to speak, they looked hurriedly between one another.

"No need to fear, Mister Secretary," said Gustav as he walked forward to take a bundle that one of the figures held in its arms. Unrolling the green and blue robe, Gustav removed his suit jacket. After pulling the robe over his head, he then took the mask that the other still held. He approached the Secretary of State before putting the mask over his face.

"What you are witnessing is the inevitable approach of a power that is much older and much stronger than anything this country has ever experienced." His voice seemed to be amplified as it came through his mask. "However, before that power can take hold, the weak foundation that is America must be swept away. It begins with the murder of your beloved President!"

The Secretary of State's eyes grew even wider. Somehow, he was still able to speak. "You're insane!" he exclaimed. "You'll never be able to murder the President in the middle of Washington and hope to get away with it!"

Gustav stepped closer until his mask was almost touching the other man's face.

"Oh, my friend, it will not be I who murders the President."

Dan's breathing began to come faster. He felt his right index finger twitch. Whatever they'd drugged him with seemed to be wearing off.

They underestimated my Midwestern metabolism, he thought to himself. He tried to flex his right hand as it hung at his side. The index finger twitched again, followed by his middle finger. He willed his hand to move, but it still wouldn't obey. Straining, Dan focused on curling his hand into a fist.

Before he could do anything else, the two main doors exploded open and the gigantic form of Otto came flying into the room. The masked assassins yelled and sprung into action, some moving to grab the Cabinet members while others ran towards the doors, leaping over Otto.

Charging into the gallery came the Chief Director of the FBI, a silver .38 in his raised right hand. He dropped the first attacker with a well-placed shot in the chest. The second attacker attempted to dodge to the left, but the Chief shot the assassin in the knee and then kicked him square in the face. A third robed figure came in from the right and tried to wrest the gun out of the Chief's hand. The Chief grappled with his assailant, keeping one hand on his gun. Turning with the assassin, the Chief saw the three cases standing in the middle of the gallery. Aiming as best he could with the attacker's hand on his wrist, he squeezed off another shot.

The bullet zipped through the air for a split second before it connected with the glass near Dan's head. The case shattered instantly as the bullet smashed through the front of the display case and out the back, narrowly missing Dan's right ear. The platform Dan was standing on gave way and he tumbled to the ground.

Dan landed on his right shoulder and rolled. All of his motor functions seemed to return as soon as he was free of the case. Pulling the mask off his face, he lunged for the nearest robed figure, who was attempting to drag the Secretary of Defense to one of the gallery's side doors. The Cabinet member was struggling as much as he could, but Dan could tell he was overmatched.

Tackling the robed assassin to the floor, Dan rolled the man over and punched him directly in the solar plexus. The Secretary of Defense fell to the floor and stayed there. The figure in Dan's grasp exhaled loudly. Standing up, Dan grabbed the dagger from its hiding place in the man's sash and turned towards the main doors.

The Chief had won the battle with the assassin who'd tried to take his gun from him. The robed figure lay motionless at his feet as the Chief kicked another one who had gotten too close. Dan ran up, grabbed that figure from behind, and stabbed him through the neck.

"Fowler!" the Chief exclaimed as the robed body fell to the floor. "About time you jumped in."

"Sorry Chief," Dan replied, "I was a bit tied up. How did you know it was me in that case?"

"I'd recognize those broad shoulders anywhere," the Chief smiled.

Dan turned to block the attack of an assailant who had a dagger in his hand. Dan stabbed the assassin in the chest and kicked him backwards, but the dagger stuck in the rough fabric of the man's robes.

The Chief shot another assailant who ran forward and then moved towards the cases that held Sally and Larry.

"Where's Berengar?" he shouted as he made his way to the display.

Dan engaged with another masked menace, dodging backwards to avoid a dagger swipe. Responding with an upper cut, Dan connected with the man's jaw under the mask and sent him to the floor.

"Which one?" Dan yelled back.

"Either one!" the Chief replied.

Taking the butt off his gun, the Chief smashed the case that held Sally. As the glass fell to the floor, she toppled forward into the Chief's waiting arms.

"I got you Vane, I got you." He pulled the mask off of her face and pushed her hair back from her eyes. She smiled groggily.

"Thanks, Chief," she mumbled.

Dan ran forward to free Larry from his glass enclosure, but was stopped as another robed attacker grabbed his right arm. Ducking a punch, Dan threw his right elbow into the man's stomach and then hooked his right arm under the man's crotch. Lifting him up, Dan threw the man directly at the case that held Larry. The case shattered, sending glass everywhere, and both Larry and the robed assassin crashed to the floor.

Pushing the unconscious figure off of him, Larry sat up and pulled the mask off of his face. "You couldn'ta done that any different, Dan?" he asked with some disgust.

"Sorry pal, I work with what I got," Dan retorted.

Dan watched as the remaining assailants fled through various doors throughout the gallery. Several robed figures lay dead around the gallery, and after a quick glance, Dan accounted for all the Cabinet members. The Secretary of State was trying to pick himself up off the floor, his arms and legs shaking as he did so.

"Mister Secretary," said Dan and he moved to help the man stand up. "Are you okay?"

The Secretary blinked at him for a moment before he recognized him. "Fowler? What in the hell is going on here? Where is Gustav?"

"I'm not sure, sir," Dan replied, "on either account. But I assure you, we will find both him and Heinrich."

"Uh, Dan?" came Larry's voice from behind him.

"Yeah?"

"Where did Otto go?"

Dan turned to where Otto had lain. The spot was empty, but a trail of blood led back towards the front entrance.

"That's not good," Dan remarked.

"I shot the big fella when he tried to attack me," said the Chief as he came up to put a hand on the Secretary's shoulder. "But he just kept coming. I had to hit him with a that." The Chief pointed to the main doors, and Dan could see a golden stanchion, intended to hold a velvet rope, lying on the marble floor. The base of it was covered in blood.

"I don't know how he got up after that," the Chief added.

"Believe me, I've seen him get up from worse," Dan replied. "But where would he have gone?"

Sally gasped and covered her mouth with her hand.

"What, Sal?" Larry asked.

Sally stared at all of them as she lowered her hand.

"The White House," she whispered. "They're going after the President."

Larry reached the car first. Still wearing the ceremonial robes, he bent down next to the driver's side door and reached underneath the vehicle. Finding the secret compartment near the wheel well, he pulled out a set of keys.

"I may not have my pants, but don't ever let them tell you Larry Kendal is without a plan!" He smiled as he unlocked the door to the large, reinforced vehicle. He unlocked the front passenger seat for Dan, and then the rear doors for Sally and the Chief.

"Where did Otto go?"

"I can't believe we don't have our clothes," said Dan as he adjusted his robe while settling into his seat.

"I'm happy to leave my dress behind," Sally replied from the backseat, shifting her own robe. "As long as we can get our hands on some guns."

"I'm prepared there as well," added Larry as he flipped a switch on the dashboard near the radio. In front of Dan, a compartment dropped open, revealing an identical .357 revolver to the one he always carried. Next to it was Larry's weapon of choice, a .38 pistol. In the rear where Sally and the Chief sat, two compartments set into the back of the front seats popped open, the first showcasing a pearl-handled .25 automatic pistol and the second a .357 revolver. Everyone reached for their preferred weapons and a box of ammo. Sally loaded her shiny .25 and smiled.

"Whaddya say, Chief?" she asked. "Do you suppose this calls for a departure from normal bureau procedure?"

The Chief put his .38 into the compartment, took out the .357, and loaded six rounds into the revolver. Snapping the chamber shut, he gritted his teeth and leaned forward.

"You're damn right it does. Step on it, Kendal."

Larry started the car, shifted into first, and peeled away from the curb.

About five minutes later, they saw the White House come into view. Approaching from the east, they didn't see any other cars or pedestrians on the streets. Larry slowed about a block from the entrance and leaned forward over the steering wheel.

"That all seem a little too dark to you?" he asked.

Dan peered forward as well. There were no lights on in the mansion, and the grounds seemed very still. In the moonlight, a single car could be seen parked in front of the south entrance.

"I'd have to agree with you there," he replied. "Look, Heinrich's car."

As their car approached the open gate off of 15th Street, four figures stepped out of the shadows to block the way. Dressed in robes, they held curved blades that glinted. All-too-familiar masks covered their faces.

"These guys again?" Sally asked from the backseat.

"This time we have old Betsy," Larry remarked, patting the car's dashboard. Shifting gears quickly, he sped towards the robed figures. Dan rolled down his window and leaned out, gun in hand. The figures didn't move until the last second, when they sprang out of the way. From the bushes lining the entrance, more robed assailants leapt onto the car, two landing on top and two on the back.

Turning his body, Dan fired a round at the figure closest to him.

The bullet caught the man square in the neck and he went tumbling to the ground, rolling several feet before he lay still. The two on the back attempted to smash the back windshield with the hilts of their scimitars, but the reinforced glass held strong. The remaining figure on top of the car attempted to move to the front, but a quick swerve from Larry sent him sprawling into the grass. His head hit the ground awkwardly and he didn't move.

Sally rolled her window down quickly and slid her petite upper body outside the car. The figure closest to her attempted to grab her, but she knocked his hand aside and grabbed his wrist. With surprising strength, she pulled the robed man off the car and sent him flying onto the lawn. Sally aimed her pistol at the other robed attacker and fired a round into his chest. Flailing backwards, he landed on the driveway and didn't get up.

Speeding around the South Lawn, Larry screeched to a stop next to Heinrich's car. All four of them spilled out of the vehicle and rushed up the stairs to the main door. Dan kicked it open and ran inside. Larry came behind, two flashlights in his hand. He gave one to Dan and surveyed the entrance with his own.

Scanning the oval room they were in, Dan saw two bodies lying on the floor a few feet away. Moving to them, he saw that they were Secret Service. Checking for pulses, he saw the long slashes across their throats, blood pooling on the floor next to them.

"Dead." He spied empty hip holsters. "Their guns are gone."

"Let's hope they misplaced them," added the Chief as he surveyed the inside of the Presidential home. Through the door in front him was a long hallway, extending to both the left and the right. Beyond the hallway sat the north entrance to the White House.

"This way," said the Chief, walking slowly into the hallway. Dan came behind him with his flashlight, his gun at eye level. Larry came next, followed by Sally. Turning left, they traversed the hallway until they came to a staircase.

"Doesn't seem to be anyone down here," Sally whispered, bringing up the rear. Moonlight streamed through the windows, casting strange shadows on the hallway carpet. Dan stopped at the base of the stairs and aimed his flashlight up the steps. The staircase turned before it reached the second floor. Larry and the Chief stopped a few paces ahead of him and surveyed the rest of the hall.

"My gut says they're up there," Dan said, quietly.

"Then let's follow your gut," Larry replied.

Slowly mounting the first step, Dan began to ascend the stairs. He kept his revolver aimed upwards, should anything suddenly come down the stairs towards him.

By the time he reached the second floor, he could feel his pulse begin to quicken. He took a few deep breaths as he peered around the second floor hallway. Doors lined the hall in either direction, and no light could be seen. Two more Secret Service members lay slumped against the far wall, their throats opened from ear to ear.

Larry, the Chief, and Sally came up behind Dan, their eyes and guns moving across their surroundings. Just then, a door to their left swung up and out came three robed assassins, daggers in hand. They stood in a line, blocking the hall, their masked eyes staring straight ahead.

"Fellas, I'm getting real tired of this," Dan spoke. "If you just tell me where Gustav and Heinrich are, you're free to go."

The robed figures made no movement save for a slight twitch from their hands, their daggers glinting in the moonlight. Suddenly, they sprang forward, coming straight at the four federal agents. Dan dropped to one knee and squeezed off a shot, catching the middle assassin square in the chest. Sally fired her pearl-handled pistol, the bullet slamming into the wooden mask of the man on the left. Larry fired his gun at the man on the right, but only winged him in the left arm. The figure kept coming and leapt at Larry, his dagger high above his head.

The blast from the Chief's .357 was like a wrecking ball hitting the man in the chest. His momentum was violently reversed by the force of the bullet, and he crashed to the floor and lay still next to the other two assailants.

"Thanks, Chief," Larry exhaled, wiping a bead of sweat from his brow.

"Sure thing, Kendal," the Chief replied. "Aim better next time."

The four agents stepped over the prone figures on the carpet and continued down the hall. No more doors swung open, and the one or two that were ajar on either side of the hallway led into empty rooms. As they neared the end of the corridor, only two doors remained – one on the left and one on the right.

Dan, still in the lead, motioned for Larry and the Chief to take the one on the right, while he and Sally took the one to their left. Holding the doorknob at the same time Larry gripped his, Dan made a silent three-count, and then turned.

Before he could open the door completely, a massive form slammed into him and drove him back into the hallway. Sally screamed and jumped out of the way, as Dan crashed into the back of the Chief, who connected with Larry, knocking him through the door he had just opened.

Sally ran into the room after them. Directly in front of her stood a four-poster bed, along with a Victorian-inspired table and set of chairs. Above the table hung a large crystal chandelier, its bulbs burning brightly. Seated in one of the chairs at the table was Gustav Berengar. In the chair opposite Gustav sat a man with short brown hair that had touches of gray. He had deep blue eyes, and a pair of rimless oval glasses sat on his strong nose. Dressed in green silk pajamas, a blanket was draped over his lap, and resting on his shoulder was the barrel of German pistol. Heinrich stood behind the seated man, his hand on the man's other shoulder.

Picking themselves up off the floor, Dan, Larry, and the Chief quickly trained their guns on the hulking form of Otto, who had also risen. The Chief looked to his right, noticing the men seated at or standing near the table. His eyes grew wide.

"Mr. President!"

Dan and Larry turned to where the Chief was staring. Sitting in the chair in front of Heinrich was Franklin Delano Roosevelt.

"You monsters," Dan said through clenched teeth.

Gustav held up a hand and smiled. "We intended to secure Herr Roosevelt at the gala tonight, but it seems, by his attire, that he had no intention of attending. So, as you Americans would say, we went to plan bee. Unfortunately, the First Lady was not at home when we called."

"Lucky for you," muttered the Chief.

Dan aimed his gun directly at Gustav's head. Larry did the same with his gun, but at Heinrich.

"And what's to stop me from shooting you where you sit, Gustav?" Dan inquired.

Gustav closed his eyes and shook his head, still smiling. "You are so brave, Herr Fowler, yet so foolish. While you and your friends may kill me and my son, you will never bring Otto down before he crushes your beloved President's skull."

Otto smiled wide at that remark and stared at Dan. He moved next to the chair where the President sat and crossed his massive arms.

"You kraut bastards will never leave here with the President," said the Chief. "You'll have to kill all of us to get out of here."

"Very well," Gustav replied. Pulling his mask from behind his back, he put it on over his face and stared at the Chief.

"What... in the..." The Chief felt his arms fall to his sides and go stiff.

"No!" screamed Dan as he squeezed off a shot at Gustav. The German moved with incredible speed to dodge the bullet. However, at the same time, Sally leveled her pistol at the chandelier above the table and fired. The bullet sped upward, breaking the chain that held the hanging fixture in place.

Gustav and Heinrich screamed as they leapt out of the way. Gustav's mask went flying off of his face and to the floor. Otto, his instincts kicking in, leaned his hulking frame forward to protect Heinrich. He took the brunt of the falling chandelier in the back of the head and the neck. In doing so, he slammed into the President's chair, causing the seated man to go sprawling forward. The rest of the chandelier smashed into the table, sending crystal shards everywhere. The Chief, suddenly able to move again, leapt forward to catch President Roosevelt before he connected with the carpet, shielding the President's body with his own.

Heinrich made a dash for the door, but found Sally blocking his path. He swung his right fist at her head. Sally ducked and brought her left fist into the young German's side. Feeling his ribs crack, Heinrich screamed in pain, but still swung wildly with his left hand. Sally dodged that blow as well and smashed the butt of her gun directly into Heinrich's jaw. He stumbled backwards and hit one of the posts on the bed, cracking the antique wood. Sally came at him, and with a swift kick to the chest, sent him crashing through the wooden upright, off of the edge of the bed, and onto the floor, where he lay motionless.

Larry moved to grab Gustav, who had sprawled to the floor as the chandelier came down, but the old man was on his feet before Larry could gain the advantage. The German swung his right fist and connected with Larry's jaw. Larry hit the floor hard and his gun flew out of his hand. Gustav attempted to jump over the prone agent, but recovering quickly, Larry reached up and grabbed his legs, bringing the German crashing to the floor. Larry quickly got on top of the other man and pinned his arms to the floor.

"That wasn't very nice, my German friend," Larry said through gritted teeth. He punched Gustav square in the face, knocking the man unconscious.

Dan moved past the Chief and the President, still on the floor, to engage with a stunned Otto. As he brought his gun to bear on the larger man, Otto swung a massive hand and sent the tabletop that was covered in crystal shards flying directly at Dan's head. Seeing this, the Chief wrapped his arms around President Roosevelt and rolled him out of the way. Covering his face, Dan felt pieces of sharp crystal cut through his robe and into his flesh. A split second later, the tabletop slammed into his forearms, sending him sprawling backwards to the floor.

As Dan tried to stand, Otto was right on top of him. He grabbed Dan in a bear hug, attempting to squeeze the life out of him. Struggling against the pressure, Dan was able to get his right arm free. He brought the butt of his revolver down on Otto's skull, momentarily stunning the large man. Otto's grip loosened, and Dan dropped to the floor. He brought his gun up, but Otto swatted wildly, knocking the firearm away. The large man then swung with a big right hook, but Dan was able to duck and avoid the oncoming fist. Swinging with a firm uppercut, Dan socked Otto in the jaw. The big man's head snapped back, but he stayed on his feet.

Unarmed, Dan continued his attack with his fists. He punched Otto in the stomach, but it felt like hitting a steel plate. He gave a second swing, connecting with solid muscle, but before he could attempt a third, Otto's giant fist cracked him across the jaw. Dan went flying to his right, nearly connecting with the bedroom wall.

Otto leaned down to grab a large piece of the wooden bedpost that lay on the floor. As he did, Sally trained her gun on him. She squeezed off a shot that hit the large German in the shoulder. Turning his attention to Sally, he took a step towards her and swung his new club, hitting her directly in the left side of the face. She crashed to the floor and didn't move.

Larry jumped up to attack the massive man, but as he ran forward, Otto turned and threw the bedpost like a javelin. The blunt end of the solid wooden beam connected with Larry's chest, sending him to the floor. He writhed in pain, trying to catch his breath.

The Chief had gotten to his feet and was aiming his gun at the gargantuan German. He fired a shot that Otto took in the chest, but before the Chief could cock the hammer back on his revolver and fire again. Otto barreled forward. President Roosevelt covered his head as the Chief went flying over him and crashed into the wall.

Dan shook his head to clear the cobwebs, his jaw screaming with pain. Pushing himself to his elbows, he saw Otto reach down and pick up Gustav's wooden mask from the floor. The big man stalked towards Dan, the large, heavy mask in his right hand. Dan tried to move backwards, but found himself against the wall. Keeping his eyes on the massive form coming at him, Dan felt around for anything he could use as a weapon. His right hand landed on something cold and metallic that felt familiar in his hand. Without thinking, he gripped the item and brought it to aim on Otto.

The room echoed with the first shot from the .357 revolver. The bullet shattered the end of the mask as Otto swung it downwards, sending splinters into his eyes. The big German recoiled, but still came forward, his wooden weapon now shortened by a few inches. Dan cocked the hammer and fired again, this time hitting Otto square in the chest. The large man stumbled, but stayed upright.

The enormous man gave a deafening bellow as he came at Dan once more. Dan fired again. The bullet sped into Otto's open mouth and through the back of his skull. Bone, blood, and hair exploded outward. The large German teetered on his feet for a second, and then fell forward. Dan rolled to his right as the colossal man came crashing down to the floor next to him, the room shaking with the impact.

Brushing himself off, Dan stood and stepped over the inert mass on the carpet. He nudged Otto's lifeless body with his foot.

"The bigger they are, I guess."

Dan moved to help Larry, who was still struggling to catch his breath, to his feet. The Chief had also found his feet, and was helping the President onto the bed. Dan then saw Sally, who was still lying on the floor, bleeding.

"Sally!" he exclaimed, letting go of Larry as his friend found a seat next to the President.

Dan knelt down and gently picked up Sally's head. Her eyes fluttered open as she came to. Seeing Dan, she gave a slight smile.

"Well hello, Mr. Fowler. Fancy meeting you here."

Dan returned her smile, but only half-heartedly as he saw the blood on the side of her head, matting down her blonde hair.

"How yah feeling, Sal?" he asked.

"Nothing a few shots of whiskey can't fix."

Dan laughed. "We'll have to ask Bert when we get back to the Bureau. Can you stand?"

"I think so, as long as I have you to help me."

"You got it."

Standing up slowly, Dan and Sally turned towards the four-poster bed.

"Agent Fowler," began President Roosevelt, "I can't thank you enough for what you and your friends have done here today."

"Just doing my duty, Mr. President," Dan replied.

Roosevelt nodded as he looked around the room at the bodies of the three Germans. Blood had pooled around Otto's head, and Gustav and Heinrich were both still unconscious, only breathing every few seconds. "I did not think these types of threats could come so close," the President continued, "let alone into my very home, but tonight has reminded me that we must be ever vigilant when dealing with such evil."

"Well said, Mr. President," added the Chief. "Hopefully, with agents such as Dan Fowler around, such evil will never again set foot on American soil."

"Agreed," replied the President. "You're a true asset to the Bureau, Agent Fowler. As are the rest of you. I hope you'll be around for a very long time."

"I plan to be, Mr. President. I plan to be. And we'll get right back to it, just as soon as Sally and I here take a little vacation out west."

Sally smiled up at Dan as she leaned against his side. "And you think this city girl wants to go west with you, Dan Fowler?"

Dan looked down at her and returned the smile. "Just for a few days, Miss Vane. I promise to have you back in time for Christmas."

Sally responded with her musical laugh. Larry added his own chuckle, as did the Chief and the President. Dan grinned wider and wrapped his arm tighter around Sally's petite frame.

"Wouldn't want you missing this city too much!'"

THE END

Dan Fowler Story Inspiration

As I set out to write my story, I wasn't sure where to begin. I'd never really written anything with existing or established characters, and I was afraid that I'd quickly get off the mark of what a "good" pulp story should be (especially since this was the first pulp story I'd ever written). I used the information I'd been given to gain a better understanding of the characters, and to create somewhat of a framework, or "skeleton," of how I saw them and what sort of characteristics they would (and should) have. Archetypes definitely played a part when starting, with the stalwart hero, the faithful sidekick, and the beautiful, intriguing woman. As far as the story itself, I knew I wanted to have it take place in the nation's capital, especially given that it was the 1930s, a somewhat tumultuous time in the world.

The idea for the artifact exhibit in the middle of Washington, D.C., put on by a noble German family, came about through another "pulp-inspired" hero—Indiana Jones. If the Germans were digging in the desert for artifacts in the years before World War II, then why couldn't a family such as the Berengars have access to mysterious relics from other parts of the world, with this relic being one that had been passed down through the generations? I've always enjoyed mysticism and superstitions in stories, and the ancient mask of Mesud seemed to fit well into a story about a federal agent battling the forces of evil in America's capital, and the idea of the Germans infiltrating D.C. through nefarious means.

Once I had my MacGuffin, I was able to frame the story around it, its supposed power, and how Dan and his friends would overcome those who would seek to use that power to achieve their evil ends. The story definitely became easier to write once I'd established where everything would take place, how the mask would be used, and how Dan, Larry, and Sally would be drawn, albeit unwillingly, into the Germans' plans. I knew I wanted the story to end at the White House, given its symbolic significance, as well as who occupied it during this time in history.

In the end, I thoroughly enjoyed writing this story, and I was very surprised at where it took me as I progressed through each page. I attempted to balance action with emotion, and hopefully provide the reader with compelling characters, whether they knew of them before this or not. Above all, I aimed to capture the reader's attention and entertain them, if only for a short bit, but you'll have to be the one to tell me if I was successful!

AARON POWERS - was born and raised in central Nebraska. He graduated from Holdrege High School in 2003, and received his Bachelor's degree in English: Writing and Literature from Wayne State College in Wayne, NE in 2007. He and his wife Abbie moved to Massachusetts in 2007, where Aaron worked as a design and editorial assistant in Boston until 2010.

After moving to Loveland, Colorado in 2010, Aaron worked as a freelance writer and editor, and published his first novel, *Children of Light: Book One: The Silver-Haired Boy*, in 2014. His first comic book story was featured in *Front Range Tales, Volume 1* in 2018. He is currently employed as a Lead Content Marketing Specialist at Madwire in Fort Collins. He loves traveling, writing, watching movies, reading comic books, playing video games, and drinking craft beer.

FAMILY AFOUL
by Fred Adams, Jr.

BIGGS, IOWA, JULY 12, 1937

The big red Buick Roadmaster rolled to a stop at the lone traffic signal in the city of Biggs, Iowa, a county seat in the middle of five thousand square miles of head-high corn in the southwestern corner of the state. The town looked sleepy, maybe because most of the locals were out driving tractors. A dozen pigeons were pecking listlessly at trash in the gutter.

Arvin Guthrie let out the clutch gently and the Buick rolled through the intersection and pulled to the curb a block from the Farmers' Bank of Iowa. It didn't look like much of a bank, but the town didn't look like much of a town either. The bank was one of two buildings on Main Street taller than two stories. The other was the Lincoln hotel, all of four floors. The tallest structure in town was the grain silo four blocks away.

Beside him, his older brother, Wendell, stared straight ahead through the windshield, his jaw working a quid of Mail Pouch. He pulled his hat low over his eyes, tucking his forelock of the family's trademark straw-blond hair under it. People who saw the posters hanging in every post office would have known him anyway by the family nose, square and downturned like an eagle's beak, pointing at his dimpled, unshaven chin. Beside him was Billy Bates, a boyhood friend taken in by the Guthrie family when he was orphaned at the age of eight.

In the back, cousin Carlene Veatch and her twin brother Ernest rode with Duane Guthrie, the youngest of the brothers.

Billy got out of the car, buttoned his suit coat over a big cowboy Colt and sauntered up the block, pausing to look into store windows. He passed the bank, casually looking through the doors. He scratched his left ear, a signal that the coast was clear.

Carlene climbed out of the car and opened the trunk. She was short and busty, her curly dark hair combed in a white-line center part. A flowered dress and T-strap shoes made her look like any young mother. She opened the trunk of the car and pulled out a pram to complete the charade. Swaddled in the blanket was a doll, and under the doll were guns.

Wendell nodded and spat. "Let's go."

Carlene and Duane led the way, Carlene pushing the baby carriage. When they reached the entrance to the bank, Billy turned around and started back in their direction. Duane wore trousers with suspenders over a white shirt, sleeves rolled to the elbows in the July heat. No place to hide a gun.

Wendell fell in fifty feet behind them. He wore bib overalls over long underwear and a sweat-stained wide-brimmed hat, looking every inch the Iowa farmer. The bank's door opened, and a bald man in a grey suit and a bow tie stepped out, looking as if he were going to a Chamber of Commerce meeting. He saw Carlene pushing the stroller and politely stepped aside, holding the door for her. Carlene smiled and Duane nodded acknowledgment.

They stepped through and the bald man turned up the sidewalk. He got three steps before he passed Billy, who nodded to him, and as an afterthought, slugged him with the Colt, laying the back of his head open. Billy giggled and crouched beside him.

Carlene and Duane stepped into the cool dimness of the Farmers' Bank lobby. A half dozen customers were queued at three of the teller windows. The uniformed guard inside the door smiled at the young couple as benignly as had the bald man, but Duane could feel his cold appraising stare. When Duane asked Wendell why he would choose a bank with a guard, Wendell said, "Hell, a bank ain't got no guard ain't go no money *to* guard."

Most guards he'd ever encountered were tired old cops. This guy looked like he might be a handful. He was younger, big, lots of muscle going to fat, straining his uniform. He wore his pistol in an open holster like a gunslinger and leaned against the wall in a casual, almost arrogant pose, as if he were daring someone to start trouble.

Wendell quick-stepped through the door behind them a few seconds later. He approached the guard and said, "Mister, there's a fella layin' on the sidewalk outside. I think he's been hurt."

The guard ran out the door, and Carlene, Duane, and Wendell reached under the blankets in the pram. Wendell pulled out a sawed-off shotgun, Carlene a .45 automatic, and Duane a cut down riot gun.

On the sidewalk, Billy knelt beside the bald man. He said, as the guard came running, "Officer, this man's hurt. He needs help." Billy turned the wrong way, and the civilian's wallet fell from his coat to the sidewalk.

Their eyes locked, and something clicked between Billy and the guard, who instinctively went for his revolver. He was fast but had spent too much time practicing his draw and not enough time shooting straight. His first bullet creased Billy's shoulder, but before he could fire again, Billy's Colt boomed and a slug punched through the front of the guard's khaki shirt and out the back. Behind him a woman screamed, and he spun and fired reflexively, separating her leg from her hip.

Inside, Carlene fired her pistol into the ceiling. She shouted, "This is a stick up. Nobody move."

Wendell saw a teller reach under the counter. "I hear an alarm bell, I start shooting people." He grabbed a young woman in a sundress by the neck and put the shotgun under her chin. "Starting with her. All of you in the cages; step back and show me your hands."

Carlene rolled the carriage through a swing gate and behind the counter. She waved her pistol at the tellers. "Fill 'er up, boys and girls." She rolled the pram down the line and the tellers threw handfuls of money into it like the collection basket at a camp meeting.

Duane had the manager at gunpoint. Let's go in the vault." Carlene followed them, pushing the pram.

Outside, Arvin swore and slammed the steering wheel with his fist. "That fool." He popped the clutch and the Buick swooped in front of the bank, hiding the dead guard but not the woman, who lay in her pooling blood. The empty street was quickly full of people pointing and shouting.

A siren, and not far away.

Ernest jumped out of the back with the Thompson and fired a burst that blew the glass out of windshields and store windows and scattered the pigeons. The bystanders ducked behind cars or flattened themselves on the sidewalk.

Inside, Wendell heard the gunfire. "Come on," he snapped at Carlene. Duane swung the barrel of his shotgun and caught the manager across the side of his face sending blood and teeth flying across the vault. He, Carlene and Wendell ran out the front door to see a black and white police car, lights flashing and siren screaming, bearing down on them.

In ten seconds, the whole plan had gone to hell.

Wendell fired one barrel then the other at the car, taking out the driver's side of the windshield. The car veered hard right and crashed into a telephone pole. Wendell threw down the shotgun and grabbed Carlene's pistol from her hand. "Go! Go!"

The passenger door opened, and a cop scrambled from the wrecked car, gun in hand. Wendell dropped him with two shots. Duane opened the trunk and threw the pram into it. He slammed the lid and dived into the back seat. Carlene piled in beside him. Ernest fired another burst from the Thompson and jumped into the car. Billy and Wendell were last. Arvin floored the gas pedal and the Buick roared up Main Street and out of Biggs.

Suddenly the street was quiet again until the screaming started.

Arvin pushed the Buick to eighty-five as they sped up the two lane blacktop. He hissed at Billy between his teeth, "Why'd you have to shoot the cop?"

"Hey, Billy said, he went for his gun. What was I going to do?"

"And that woman?"

"I didn't know what was going on. I —"

"Both of you shut up." Wendell's thick voice stopped the argument like the slamming of a door. "Lemme think."

"We got the money and we got away," Carlene said. "What else is there?"

"I said shut up."

The Guthries had been in the bank robbing business for nearly a year, since the Depression eased up and the banks started having money in them again. They had robbed eight, including today's heist, but no one had gotten killed — up to now. He wasn't sure what was worse, killing the woman — he was sure she was dead — or killing the cop. They weren't just bank robbers anymore, they were killers, and that meant the noose in Iowa, maybe for all of them.

Carlene was right. They had the money but for Wendell and his brothers, the money was a secondary consideration. The Guthries were out to make the banks pay. They foreclosed on the family's Kansas farm when the crops failed, and when the Sheriff's deputies came with that man in the suit. Patriarch Samson Guthrie, drunk as often as not, raised hell. He went in the house and came back out with his shotgun, and all three deputies shot him dead in front of his family. It didn't matter that the shotgun was empty.

Samson had no money to buy shells.

They might as well have shot Mama too. She died six months later of a broken heart.

Wendell didn't blame the deputies. What bothered him was the smug grin on the man in the suit, banker Robert "call me Bob" Albright, and the greedy gleam in his eyes as he saw his fortunes increase. At that moment, Wendell Guthrie decided that he would make The Bank pay for his father's death. Not just First National, Albright's bank, but "The Bank" as a predatory vulture perched in a crooked tree waiting for families to die. He vowed to make them bleed green as long as he had breath in his lungs.

Arvin watched the odometer. At exactly five and three-tenths miles, he slowed to a stop. Billy and Duane jumped out. Each took an end of a length of wire mesh fencing with stalks of corn threaded through the squares. Arvin drove the car through the opening and bumped and rumbled over the furrows and rocks until the car was hidden from the road. Arvin shut off the engine and climbed out.

It took about five minutes of searching through the rows of corn, but he found what he was looking for; a Reo pickup truck orange with rust, bales of hay stacked in the bed, and a Model T flivver that they'd hidden there the day before.

When he got back to the Buick, Ernest and Carlene were scooping money from the pram and loading it into a canvas tool bag. Wendell was buttoning a chambray work shirt over his overalls. He switched his felt hat for a straw one and slipped on a pair of steel rimmed eyeglasses. Billy was changing from his suit to farm clothes.

Duane scooped handfuls of hay from the center of a bale to hide the money and the guns. He, Arvin, Carlene and Ernest would ride together in the Model T with a picnic basket on the back seat, just friends on an outing if they were stopped. Billy would ride with Wendell in the Reo.

Wendell heard the drone of an engine. He shielded his eyes and saw a red and yellow biplane coming, a white stream billowing from its tail.

"Quick," Duane shouted. "Get out of sight."

"Too late, damn it." Wendell growled.

The biplane finished a pass and swung in a lazy arc. The pilot, wearing a leather helmet with goggles looked over the lip of his cockpit and waved a gloved hand. He circled back for another pass.

"He doesn't know what's happened yet," Wendell said. "But as soon as he does, he'll figure out who we are. We'd better get out of here."

"Stick to the plan?" Arvin said.

"Hell, yes, stick to the plan. Quick, get moving before he comes back around."

He climbed into the Reo and stepped on the starter. The engine sprang to life almost instantly. It looked like a rickety bucket of bolts, but Arvin had tuned and souped up the engine to make it as fast as any prowl car. Billy climbed into the cab, avoiding Wendell's eyes. He recognized the cold fury in Wendell's manner without a word or gesture. He knew he had screwed up, and wasn't sure where that left him in Wendell's estimation.

Wendell would drive the truck through the corn to the northeast where he would join township road 317 and turn left. Arvin would drive the flivver, top down, to the southeast and follow 317 in the opposite direction where they would turn onto a local road to a park. They would wait out the initial frenzied dragnet then leave the park and follow another dirt road across the border into Kansas, where they would rendezvous and head for the hideout.

When the crop duster flew over again, he could see the bright red hump of the Roadmaster, but the car and truck, like the people, were gone.

A few miles north on 317 the Highway Patrol had set up a roadblock. Two cars sat nose to nose. Officers stood beside them, riot guns braced on their hips.

"Put your head down," Wendell said to Billy. "Pretend you're asleep." He slowed the Reo and stopped twenty feet short of the block.

A trooper put a foot on the running board and looked into the truck. The flap on his holster was unbuttoned. "Where you fellows coming from?"

"Tellis," Wendell said. He jerked a thumb over his shoulder. "Heading back to Kingwood. Hay for the cows. Something happen, officer?"

"We're looking for some people. May I see your license?"

"Sure thing." Wendell fished a cracked leather wallet from his pocket and pulled out a tattered license. As he did, he looked in the rear-view mirror and saw the two shotgun cops climbing into the bed. They were lifting the bales, looking between and under them. The cop on the running board studied the license for a minute and handed it back. "Thank you, Mister — Montrose. You see a new red Buick on the road?"

"No, sir. Saw a few cars, but no red ones."

"Is your friend okay?"

Wendell elbowed Billy, who jumped a little and blinked his eyes. "Liam, wake up."

"Wha—?" Billy looked confused as any waking person might.

"Say howdy to the officer."

"Uh, howdy."

One of the men in the bed said something Wendell couldn't hear, and the cop nodded. The officers jumped out of the bed of the Reo. "Drive carefully, Mister Montrose." He stepped away and one of the police cars backed out of the road. In two minutes, the road block was tiny in the rear view mirror. A minute more and it was out of sight.

"That was a close one," Billy said, turning to look out the rear window.

"No, it wasn't. It was all part of the plan."

They rode a few more miles in silence and Wendell pulled off the highway.

"Why are we stopping?"

"I think you know why." Wendell shut off the motor and stared through the cracked windshield. He held out his hand without looking at Billy. "The wallet."

"What wallet?"

"Don't bullshit me, Billy. The wallet you took from the guy you slugged. You dropped it, the guard saw it, and that made the whole works unravel. Ernest saw it hit the sidewalk. All you had to do was slug the guard when he bent over. You didn't follow the plan, and you damn near got us all killed."

Billy stared at his shoes. "I'm sorry, Wendell. I just didn't think."

"That's the trouble, Billy. You just don't think. Get out of the truck."

"What?"

"I said get out of the truck."

"No, wait a minute, Wendell, you can't just —"

"We're through, Billy. Here's where you get off." Wendell drew an automatic and thumbed back the hammer. "Get out of the truck."

Billy put up his hands. "Okay, Wendell, okay." He reached behind him for the door handle and his fingers brushed the butt of the Colt in the waistband of his pants. Ideas spun in his head. Truck. Money. Gun. He opened the door and slid off the seat. As he did, he tugged at the pistol, but the sight caught in his trousers and it jerked out all at once.

Wendell's .45 boomed like a cannon in the cab of the truck. Billy pitched out backwards and landed on the hard-packed berm.

"Damned fool," Wendell said. He put the Reo in gear and drove away, leaving Billy to bleed out in the dirt. Wendell felt no remorse. He'd given Billy a chance to walk away and to live, but Billy went his own way, like he always did. Eight more miles to the farm road that would take him across the border, and he'd be in Kansas.

WASHINGTON, D.C. JULY 13

"Good morning, Ira." Dan Fowler laid a dollar bill on the newsstand counter.

"Hi, Mister Fowler," the little man behind the counter said, reaching for a stack of newspapers. "Here you go." He laid out three, the *Washington Post*, the *New York Times*, and the *Pittsburgh Press*.

Fowler scooped up the papers and said, "Keep the change, Ira." He tucked them under his arm and looked at his watch. Plenty of time for breakfast before he went to the office.

He turned up 10th Street Northwest. The July sun was bright but not yet hot enough to make honest people sweat.

Fowler was the sort of man the average person might call imposing if not intimidating. Standing six feet four inches, his two hundred pounds of bone and muscle carried a head with a face that belied his age. The lines around his eyes and his craggy features made him appear older than his thirty-two years. His broad-shouldered, slim-hipped build filled his tan suit in a way that turned women's heads as he walked by.

Four blocks from the Bureau offices, Fowler went into Morrie's, a diner tucked between a haberdashery and a cinema. He slid into a booth and before he could open his newspapers, Marge, the waitress scurried over with a cup and saucer in one hand, and a coffee pot in the other. "What'll you have today, Mister Fowler?"

"Eggs over easy with bacon and toast, and a glass of tomato juice."

"I didn't even have to write it down," she said with a laugh, putting her pad and pencil in the pocket of her uniform. "You order the same thing every time."

"Someday, I'll surprise you, Marge."

"On the way."

He opened the *Times* first and scanned the front page. He always read the *Times* first, the *Press* for a second opinion, and finally the *Post* for the political slant. The big news was from across the pond. Prime Minister

Neville Chamberlain basically told his Japanese counterpart Fuminaro Konoe "nuts" to the Japanese demand that the Brits reverse their foreign policy in the Far East and leave China ripe for conquest. The FBI's operations were strictly stateside, and Fowler was more interested in what was happening in the U.S., particularly the Underworld, but he liked to keep up with current events.

Marge brought his platter and refilled his coffee. Fowler continued to read as he ate. A second bank robbery in Iowa in two weeks. Putting Ben and Stella Dixon behind bars didn't seem to have slowed the trade much, he thought, but that was a matter for the Omaha field office — it was on their turf — unless they got a line on a fugitive, then the phone on his desk would ring.

Dan Fowler was a Special Investigator, a manhunter who served at the pleasure of the Director. He could be called upon day or night to travel anywhere in the country to track down the worst of the worst.

As the Director put it, Fowler had "a nose for evil," and his record for apprehension rivaled the best of the Bureau. His successes had put him on the fast track for promotion and made him the youngest man in the Bureau to be promoted to the rank of Inspector, to the admiration of some, and the jealous dislike of others.

Fowler was on his second piece of toast when the diner door opened and a tall, trim man in a suit came in. It was fellow agent, Bob Martin. He scanned the patrons and spotted Fowler, who spotted him at the same time. When the newcomer didn't slide into the booth, Fowler knew he wouldn't be finishing his breakfast.

"Don't tell me," Fowler said.

"The Director needs you. He said, 'now.'"

Fowler downed the last of his juice, folded his newspapers, and left a two dollar bill under his coffee cup. "Let's go." As they walked toward Pennsylvania Avenue, Fowler asked, "Any idea what this is all about?"

"Not a clue. But the Director is pretty hot about something."

"I guess I'll find out soon enough."

In moments they were climbing the steps of the Department of Justice Building, home to the Bureau's offices and the office of the Director. Three floors up, Fowler left Martin and walked down the long hallway past the door to his own office with INSPECTOR DANIEL FOWLER in black letters on the pebbled glass. He opened the door and threw the newspapers on the desk then hung his fedora on the coat tree, straightened his necktie, and headed to see the Director.

The Director was his usual dyspeptic self, but when your job is protecting 130 million American citizens from the other .9 million, it not only came with the turf, it was the turf. "Close the door, Fowler." He did. The Director stood to the side of his desk looking out the window at the bustle below on

Pennsylvania Avenue. "Look down there. Five years ago, you didn't see the traffic. People couldn't afford a car, or if they owned one, couldn't afford gasoline or tires. The economy is recovering. Roosevelt says so every time he's on the radio. It's coming back, but it's fragile.

"But with recovery comes money, and just as people are beginning to trust the banks instead of burying their money in a coffee can in the back yard or sewing it up in a sofa cushion, the country's turning into the Wild West again."

"Bank robbers, sir?"

"Yes." The Director stared at the glowing end of his cigar. "We've managed to take down the worst of them: Dillinger, Baby Face Nelson, Pretty Boy Floyd, the Murdock brothers, but new ones keep popping up like toadstools. You've heard of the Guthrie clan." A statement, not a question.

Fowler nodded. "I've read the reports. Seven robberies in the last year, all in the Midwest."

"Eight, as of yesterday, but up to now, no one was killed. Yesterday, they shot up the town of Biggs, Iowa and killed a bank guard, two local police officers and a bystander."

"How did it all go down?"

"We're still gathering information from witnesses. What we have so far is all in there." He tapped a manila file folder with his forefinger. "These people have become a scourge as big as Ma Barker's clan. I want them stopped. Take Kendall with you." He turned his back and looked out the window.

Dismissed.

"This job was planned down to the last detail." Larry Kendall looked up from the report of the Biggs robbery. Fowler's partner stubbed out his cigarette in the ashtray beside him. Kendall, whose movie star looks and suave manner made him appear as if he'd be more at home in a country club than the FBI, sat across from Fowler, whose desk was strewn with files, photos, and maps. While Fowler was in shirtsleeves in the July heat, Kendall still wore the jacket of his tailored suit, and his flowered necktie was perfectly knotted at the collar of his crisp white shirt. He eyed the photo of Wendell Guthrie in a wanted poster. "I thought these people were Okies."

"They make up for their lack of education and sophistication with a kind of feral cunning. Maybe they're getting better with practice. Maybe now that they're Public Enemies and the heat is on them, they're being more careful. Their first few robberies were simple gun, grab, and goes. The last

"How did it all go down?"

few show some clever ploys. The pram was just shy of genius."

"But this time, the plan went south." Kendall stared at the stark photo of the pretty young woman lying on the sidewalk like a broken doll in a dark pool of blood. "Something went sideways. I wonder what."

"The Guthries have become notorious, and their pictures have been sent to every bank in the Midwest. It's not so easy for them to waltz in unnoticed. Maybe that's why all the subterfuge. The more gears in the works, the more likely it'll break down."

A knock at the door interrupted their conversation. Bob Martin opened the door and stuck his head in. "There's been a break in the Biggs investigation."

"When do we leave?" Kendall said.

"Right away."

Larry gathered the paperwork from the desk, pausing to gaze at the dead girl's photo once more. "Annie Tyler."

"Huh?"

"That was her name, Annie Tyler. Honey," Larry said, "we're going to make them pay. My word."

Fowler opened the closet and pulled out a brown leather suitcase, his travel bag, always packed and ready. "I'll meet you downstairs. I have a stop to make."

Kendall chuckled. "Give Sally my regards."

On the floor below, Fowler followed the corridor to an end office and looked in the open door.

Sally Vane sat at her desk, typing with the speed of a Tommy gun. He had to remind himself that despite her feminine beauty, Sally was an agent and was thoroughly trained in firearms and hand-to-hand self-defense. In a tight spot, she was as capable and dangerous as any man.

She looked up as Fowler came through the doorway into her office and gave him a broad smile. He crossed to her desk and sat on a corner. "Busy day?"

"Every day." She stopped typing and brushed a strand of wavy blond hair away from her forehead. "Did you order this heat?"

Fowler laughed. "Sure did. Good for the corn crop."

"Well, maybe you can scale it back a little tomorrow."

"Still doing your own typing, huh?" Despite being one of the first women accepted as an agent by the Bureau, Sally still did much of her own clerical work.

"Someday, I'll have a secretary, just like the boys. In the meantime, I can type faster than most of the girls in the Typing Pool, anyway." Sally changed the subject. "You asked about my day. How's yours?"

"Just as busy." He looked over his shoulder at the open door. "Going out of town."

"Anywhere exciting?"

"Iowa."

Her smile faded. "You're going after the Guthrie gang, aren't you?"

"Word gets around fast."

"I heard people talking about the robbery in the break room."

They're bad people, Sally. Somebody has to take them on."

"But why does it always have to be you?"

"Just lucky, I guess."

Sally gripped his hand. "You come home safe to me, Dan."

"Always, Sally." He wanted to lean over and kiss her, but fraternization between Bureau employees was frowned upon, and displays of affection taboo. He had to settle for pinching her cheek and headed for the door. "I'll call you tonight."

An hour later, Fowler and Kendall were on an Army Air Corps plane to Iowa.

"Don't forget to reset your watch," Kendall said. "We get a spare hour in the Central Time Zone."

Fowler looked out the window of the Ford C-3 at the monochrome landscape below, miles of wheat in every direction, undulating like ocean waves in the prairie wind. When do we land in Des Moines?"

"Three-thirty, but I heard one of the crew say we aren't landing at the airport."

"We're not?"

BIGGS, IOWA

The tri-motor made a pass over a mile-long stretch of highway blocked at either end by black '35 Ford sedans with the gold shield of the newly minted Iowa Highway Patrol logo on the doors.

"They've only had a highway patrol since thirty-four," Kendall said. "I hope they're up to the job. Do you suppose that's why the Guthries have robbed three banks in iowa? Inexperienced law enforcement??"

"I don't imagine the first fifty men the state swore in were plucked at random off the street," Fowler replied.

"Or off the tractor."

A sergeant walked through the passenger compartment. "Buckle your belts, gentlemen. Time to set down."

To the pilot's credit, touchdown was reasonably gentle, and the plane rolled to a stop fifty yards short of the roadblock. Fowler and Kendall climbed from the plane and felt the heat of the blacktop through the soles of their shoes.

Two men in suits strolled over. The taller one held out his hand. "Agent Edward Shaw. Which one of you is Special Agent Fowler?"

Kendall jerked a thumb at his partner. "Him. He's the famous one. I'm Kendall, the good-looking one."

"This is Agent Dean Wilcox," Shaw said. "We're from the Omaha office."

The troopers moved the patrol cars out of the way, and the C-3 swept down the highway and lifted into the sky. The pilot circled, dipped his wings and turned east.

"How far are we from Biggs?" Kendall asked.

"About five miles. We'll go there later. Right now, we'll take you to the spot where they abandoned the getaway car." They all climbed into one of the Bureau's green Pontiac sedans, what Sally always called "The Big Uglie."

"So they were seen from the air?" Fowler said as Wilcox drove them toward the site.

"Yeah; it was pure luck a crop duster pilot, local guy named Fred Barnes just started dusting a cornfield when he saw them thirty yards off the highway. It was the getaway car, a big red Buick and a group of men and a woman. They left the Buick and drove off in two other vehicles hidden in the corn close by. They went two different directions, and while the Highway Patrol was all up and down the main highway, they disappeared."

"That's new. They've traded cars before, but never splitting up."

"Yep. If Barnes hadn't seen the Buick. we'd still be looking for it."

They saw the cluster of FBI vehicles and Highway Patrol cars a mile before they reached it on the ruler straight highway. Wilcox pulled onto the berm and shut off the engine. "Let's go meet the Boss."

They walked through the opening in the wall of corn and Shaw pointed to the section of camouflaged fencing that hid the gap. "Camouflage."

"Clever," Fowler said.

"They took great pains to hide."

"And so close to the crime scene," Kendall added.

The corn was beaten flat by all the vehicles and the feet, and the curving path led to the red Buick Roadmaster. All four doors, the hood and the trunk gaped open, and men were crawling all over the car. Some dusted for fingerprints, others searched under the seats and in the glove compartment for any scrap of evidence the car might give up. Overseeing the scene was a wiry man in a seersucker suit and bow tie. His grey hair was parted severely to the right, and he wore rimless spectacles that magnified his pale blue eyes, giving them a severe intensity. His face was elongated by what Fowler figured was a full set of false teeth, and his mouth was pressed into a thin line that looked as if it had never smiled.

"Deputy Director Payden," Shaw said, and the man turned. He eyed the newcomers, and Fowler felt in that hard stare the same command presence he found in the Director. "These are the agents from D.C. This is Agent Kendall and this is Agent Fowler."

Payden eyed Kendall and Fowler up and down in turn like a cattle buyer appraising a couple of steers. "Did you get them up to speed, Walsh?"

"Yes, sir, with as much as we know."

"The Sheriff has arranged rooms for us in his station in Biggs as an operations center and the Bureau has rooms ready for them at the Lincoln hotel. Get them settled and I'll meet with all of you at the Sheriff's office in two hours."

"Sir," said Fowler, "with all due respect, may we take a look at the scene since we're already here?"

Payden took a full minute to consider the request then nodded his head. "Very well. I'll see you at the operations center." He walked away without another word.

"Is he always so personable?" Kendall said.

Wilcox nodded. "Pretty much."

"I could just see the seconds ticking off in his head," Fowler said. "Making us wait for an answer. He was letting us know who's in charge."

"Well, let's see what the lab boys have come up with." Shaw led them to the car where technicians were dusting every smooth surface for fingerprints.

"What do you think about the scientific approach?" Fowler said.

"I don't know," Shaw replied. "I'm more the old fashioned shoe leather type. The Bureau's only been doing this kind of investigation since 1930." He tapped a technician on the shoulder. "Finding any prints?"

"Plenty," the man replied. "So many that the crooks will probably die of old age before we sort them all out."

"It's a given that the Guthries pulled this job," Kendall said. "Why take the prints?"

"Just in case they had someone else in on the action," Wilcox said. "We want 'em all."

Fowler nodded. "Amen to that."

On the other side of the car men were pouring moulage casts of footprints. Kendall snorted. "All this evidence will help the prosecutors, but it won't help us find the sons of bitches."

"They split up and drove two different ways," Wilcox said. "The tire tracks will tell us at least what make and model they're driving. That could help."

"If there's nothing more to see here," Fowler said, "Let's go to headquarters."

Walsh nodded at their suitcases. "Don't you want to go to your rooms first?"

"No, I want to see what you've got. We can check in later."

WESTERN KANSAS

Wendell carried his coffee out onto the porch. The abandoned farm was a good hideout, but they'd have to find another soon. Overstaying your welcome was a bad idea. He'd sent Carlene into town for groceries, since she was the only one whose face wasn't on the post office wall. She would be soon, but for the moment, she could still move around and not be recognized.

When they rendezvoused, Duane said, "Where's Billy?" Wendell didn't answer. He'd just stood still and his stern gaze swept all their faces. No one had brought it up since. Billy was okay when they started their crusade against the Bank, but there's a difference between satisfaction and enjoyment. The more banks they robbed, the more Billy seemed to relish the risk, the excitement, and the power a gun gave him over other people.

Wendell knew he could never put the Bank out of business. It was too big, too powerful and had its tentacles into everything, but he would make it hurt as much and as long as he could.

The door opened, and Arvin came out, a beer in each hand. He sat beside Wendell and offered him one of the bottles. They'd been cooled in the spring house behind the barn and they sweated in the afternoon heat. He took a drink and rolled the bottle over his forehead.

Wendell drank half his bottle in one pull. "Done counting?"

"Four thousand, three hundred forty-one dollars and eighteen cents."

"Things are improving."

"Would have been more if you'd've let us rob the customers too."

"No. They're people just like us. I won't take their money."

It was a debate they'd had many times, but Wendell was adamant and in the Guthrie clan, his word was law. That was a reason he'd gotten rid of Billy as much as his wrecking what should have been a smooth plan and putting all their heads in a noose.

"Think maybe we ought to lay low for a while?" Arvin said. "Back off for a couple of months? Pull up stakes and relocate where people won't be looking for us — maybe Texas."

"Maybe." Wendell drank the rest of his beer. "After the next job."

Arvin nodded. He knew argument was futile. Wendell was set on his course and wasn't about to give it up easily. He looked across the field of weeds and briars and saw a dust cloud approaching. "I don't know how many times I've told Carlene to drive slow so she doesn't raise a cloud and attract attention."

The flivver rolled into the bare earth of the front yard and shuddered to a stop. Carlene climbed out of the car and ran to the porch waving a newspaper. "We're on the front page!" she shouted. "The front page of the *Evening Star!*"

Arvin took the newspaper and held it so both he and Wendell could see the front page. The boldface headline read: GUTHRIE GANG KILLS FOUR IN IOWA ROBBERY. Below the headline were mug shot photos of Wendell, Arvin, and Ernest from previous scrapes with the law.

Arvin pointed to an article below about President Roosevelt signing a farm relief bill. "Look at that. We're even bigger news than FDR. Listen to this," Arvin said as Ernest and Duane came outside. "'In a blazing gun battle Tuesday, the infamous Guthrie Gang, killed a bank guard, a bystander and two police officers in the robbery of the Biggs branch of the Farmers' Bank of Iowa. FBI Deputy Director Lyman Payden said that a 'tri-state dragnet' is in operation to find the gang and bring them to justice.'"

"I guess we're famous," Duane said.

"I guess so," Wendell said. "Put the car in the barn before somebody sees it." He stood, stretched, and walked away.

The Sheriff's Office in Biggs had a pair of rooms, one with a desk and one with a table and chairs. The windows were open and flies buzzed in and out. A large midwest regional map was tacked to the wall with pins marking the eight known Guthrie robberies.

Fowler studied the map while Shaw spoke. "We're looking at a four state area; three robberies in Missouri, two in Nebraska, two in Oklahoma, and now one in Iowa." Using a yardstick as a pointer, he drew a circle around the pins. "We're looking at an irregular pattern at best. I'd suggest they were moving around, robbing as they went, but the dates and the places don't support that. Two in Nebraska then one in Missouri, one in Oklahoma and back to Nebraska again."

"Maybe they're trying to make it look random," Kendall said, "to throw us off their trail."

"Or maybe it is really random, feeling their way along as they go."

"I doubt that," said Kendall. "The robberies seem to be too well planned. Everything they've done up to now seems to have been thought through in some detail."

"I agree," said Fowler. "I think it's a mistake to think we're dealing with a pack of ignorant hillbillies." He stood up. "If you look at the locations of the known robberies, they don't form a circle per se, as if they originate from a central location, a hideout if you will." He took the yardstick from Shaw. "But you can see two rough circles if you connect these three," he tapped three of the pins, "and these three, which coincidentally line up by date. Maybe they have changed their home base from time to time, pulled a few heists, then changed locations. And where is the state where they pulled no jobs?"

"Kansas," said Wilcox. "You think they're holed up in Kansas?"

"Great," Shaw groaned. "That narrows it down to eighty-two thousand square miles."

"If we connect the first three and the second three as rough circles. we can locate their centers with a little geometry. Both are in the western part of the state. If we imagine an arc between the most recent two, we can extend it into a full circle and its center too is in western Kansas. No bank jobs in Kansas, nobody looks for them in Kansas."

"And the Guthries are all born and raised in a wheat field. A dog doesn't shit where he sleeps," Wilcox said with a laugh.

"An aptly chosen metaphor." Everyone turned and saw Payden standing in the doorway. "Your idea has a certain amount of merit, for as far as it goes, Agent Fowler. But how can we put it to use?"

"If we calculate a rough center from the last two locations, we can determine what cities, and what banks are within that circle. If they go true to pattern, they'll hit one of them."

Payden nodded. "That's very good logic, Fowler. I think you men should pursue that angle. I just got a call from the County Sheriff, Evan Potter. He says a body was found on a farm road seventeen miles from Biggs. The dead man's been tentatively identified as Billy Bates, part of the Guthrie gang."

"They're sure it's Bates?"

Payden nodded. "He fits eyewitness descriptions, and he was still carrying the wallet stolen from Arthur Fillburn, whom he assaulted on the sidewalk outside the bank."

"Could you please show us on the map where he was found?" Fowler said.

Payden tilted his head to squint at the map through the bottom of his bifocals. "Here." He put a finger on the map.

Kendall eyed the location and whistled. He pointed to a road beside Payden's finger. "And guess where that road leads: the Kansas border."

After supper, Fowler retired to his room in the Lincoln hotel. The room was small and simple, but compared to some of the accommodations he'd endured over the past few years, it was better than average. A ceiling fan moved the dusty air that slipped through the open window and after the sun went down did a passable job of cooling the place. The hot and cold water taps in the bathroom ran at about the same temperature, but it didn't matter. He wouldn't be taking a hot bath any time soon. The mattress on the single bed was firm and mercifully not lumpy.

There was no desk in the room, but a small stand held a switch hook telephone. He put the earpiece to his ear and jiggled the hook. The switchboard operator came on and Fowler gave her Sally Vane's number in D.C.

Sally asked Fowler once why he never carried a photo of her in his wallet, and his reply was simple. "I don't need a picture. Your image is fixed in my mind for good." The real reason he didn't carry Sally's picture with him was that he didn't want her identity as an agent compromised, or for some crook to connect the two of them and use her to get to him.

After some clicks and crackles, the ring tone buzzed in his ear. One ring, two . . . "Hello?"

"That was quick. Were you holding the phone in your lap?"

She laughed. "Lucky you're a thousand miles away."

"I'll bet. How are things in D.C.?"

"Still holding together. Of course you've only been gone for a day. How's the case coming?"

For the next few minutes, Fowler gave her the lowdown on the investigation. "We may have gotten a break. One of the gang was found dead, and it looks as if he was shot by his own people."

"Really? Wow. That's something."

"More than anything the location where he was found gives some idea of their getaway path. We're hoping to find them before they strike again."

"You know what I'm going to tell you."

"Yes. I will be careful."

"You'd better, Dan." She paused. "Time to quit running up the Bureau's phone bill."

"I'll call you tomorrow."

"Goodnight, Dan." The phone clicked in his ear.

Fowler lay in his bed for a long time staring at the ceiling, watching the shadows cast by the turning fan. As he often did, he imagined the elements of the case as circles and tried to determine where they intersected, like the Venn diagrams his Philosophy professor, Doctor Van Weller used to draw on the blackboard when he was a college sophomore. Where did they overlap, share common ground, become tangent or congruent? He was sure that he was right about Kansas, but the state was full of abandoned farms, empty homesteads, and ghost towns, a result of the Depression and the drought that turned the Midwest into the Dust Bowl.

Waiting for the Guthries to pull another holdup gnawed at him, but for the moment, there was little else he could do. As the town clock chimed one, he closed his eyes and drifted off to sleep.

BIGGS, IOWA JULY 15

"We've been looking at the Guthries from the start of their crime spree," Fowler said. "Maybe we need to take a closer look at their history before they started robbing banks." He picked up a file folder. "A few of them have records that predate the robberies; Wendell did a year in Lansing Penitentiary for assaulting a police officer. So did Duane, at the same time. The cousin Ernest was arrested for burglary, but the store owner dropped the charges because Ernest was drunk and all he stole was a sack of chicken feed."

"The others are clean." Wilcox stubbed out his cigarette. "What does that tell us?"

"Nothing as unrelated fact, but they all fit into the picture somehow. I'm going to call the Sheriff in their home county and find out about the assault charges."

"The tire tracks gave us one vehicle for sure," said Shaw. "A Model T, based on the tire tread and the distance between the wheels. The other vehicle was some kind of truck. Both were probably stolen."

"Like the Buick," Kendall said. "It went missing from a car lot fifty miles away."

"So one of them knows cars." Fowler jotted a note on his pad.

"That would be Arvin Guthrie," Wilcox said. "He worked as a mechanic for a garage in Lawrence, Kansas until last October, then he turned in his notice and disappeared. Soon after, the robberies started."

"It all fits." Fowler said. "The family got together and decided to go into the stickup business. I'm going to call Asaph County and talk with the Sheriff."

When he reached the Asaph County Municipal Building, Fowler was connected to Sheriff Alvin Beck. He identified himself, and said, "I'm investigating the Biggs, Iowa bank robbery and trying to get a line on the Guthrie family. You were the Sheriff when Wendell and Duane were arrested for assaulting a police officer?"

"Nope, that was Tommy Craddock. He died last year, prostate cancer. I took over the office, but I can tell you all about it. I was one of the deputies they attacked."

Beck told Fowler about the eviction proceeding, the shooting of Samson Guthrie, and the brawl that ensued. "Damned shame Samson come at us with an empty gun, but how would we have known. We didn't want to shoot the boys, too, so we beat them down with nightsticks. Hell, I lost a tooth, and Tom Wells's left eye never has been right since. I understand why they were angry and took it out on us, but Tommy and the district attorney thought we needed to make an example of them because we were doing evictions every week, and we couldn't have people thinking we were

""Maybe we need to take a closer look at their history..."

punching bags."

"The eviction," Fowler said, "was it a bank?"

"Uh-huh. First National of Kansas was holding the paper."

"And was the eviction legitimate?"

"Sure was. Samson was four months behind on his mortgage. The judge had no option. The law is the law."

"Billy Bates; was he involved?"

"Billy Bates. Now there's a bad seed. The Guthries took him in when his parents died, and he was like one of the family. But he wasn't around that day. Don't know what ever happened to him."

"He's dead."

Beck grunted. "Just as well."

"So Wendell and Duane went to Lansing for a year. What happened to the rest of the family?"

"Arvin took Beulah, his mother to live with relatives somewhere out of state. What I understand, she died soon after, and none of us has seen hide nor hair of any of 'em since."

"And the bank, First National, where is the branch located?"

"I can see it out my window. Still in business."

"Thanks for the information, Sheriff. I'll be in touch." Fowler hung up the phone. The family homestead lost, father killed, mother died, and two of the three sons jailed. It all connected somehow, but it was still too vague an outline. Time to see what the others on the team came up with.

He walked into the conference room and found Shaw and Kendall reading a newspaper over Wilcox's shoulder. The headline read: GUTHRIES STILL AT LARGE; FBI STUMPED.

Beside a picture of the Biggs carnage, the article sported a photo of Payden, looking official. The subheading was FBI HAS NO ANSWERS.

"Sometimes I think these newspapers root for the bad guys," Kendall said.

"Naah," Wilcox set the paper down. "I think they just print whatever will catch the public eye to sell newspapers."

"The Public's right to know," snorted Shaw. "If the public only knew the whole story . . ." He looked up at Fowler. "What'd you find?"

"That the assault charges stemmed from Wendell and Duane attacking three Sheriff's deputies who shot their father during an eviction procedure." He quickly recounted the details of the incident.

"I can't say that I wouldn't have reacted in the same way," Wilcox said, "if I saw somebody shoot down my dad." The others nodded in agreement.

"Dean, didn't you say that the Guthries cleaned out the vault and the cash drawers but didn't take money or valuables from the customers?"

"Yeah, that's right, and it's been the same in all the robberies."

"So they want to hurt the bank, not the everyday people."

"Everyday people like themselves." Kendall said. "Is that what you're suggesting?"

Fowler nodded. "It makes sense. The Bank with a capital B failed all these people, took their money, took their homes, everything they had. The Guthries, Wendell in particular as the head of the clan, sees the customers as fellow victims, kindred spirits."

"Let the everyday people keep their cash while the banks lose theirs." Kendall nodded. "Makes sense."

"And no harm to the customers either. Bank personnel get roughed up, including guards, but never a customer. Sounds like a vendetta."

"That shines an odd light on it all." Wilcox said. "What changed this time?"

"According to witnesses," Shaw answered, "Bates shot the guard when he came out of the bank then turned and shot the bystander."

"Their names are George Smith and Annie Tyler," Kendall said, "just so we don't stop thinking about them as people."

"Right." Shaw went on. "From that point, once the shooting started, it was a battle royal."

"And Billy Bates turns up dead later. He had two wounds, one just a graze on his shoulder, probably from the robbery. We know he was shot where we found him, not during the robbery. He was lying on a pistol the same caliber shot," he paused, "George Smith. So, did the gang shoot him for screwing things up?"

Fowler tapped his teeth with the end of his pencil. "That's an interesting thought. Let's say the Guthries didn't want to shoot anyone. They were forced into it because Billy pulled the trigger. As far as we know, it was Wendell who killed the two cops because he had to. Maybe he decided it time to get rid of Billy."

"Maybe, but this could break two ways. They could quit, or they could just become more desperate."

"But they still haven't hit the bank that killed their father, First National." Fowler put a pin into the map. "Right there. Fillburn Kansas."

WESTERN KANSAS

"He's been out there a long time, Duane." Arvin turned away from the window. Wendell had been sitting on a stump in the front yard of the farmhouse for more than an hour staring at nothing in particular.

"You want to bother him? You go ahead. I'm staying away. I don't want to end up like Billy."

"We don't know what happened to Billy."

"Oh yeah? You keep fooling yourself, Arvin. Billy messed up, and now he's gone. What if you or I mess up?"

"He'd never hurt any of us. We're family."

"Billy was family."

To that, Arvin had no answer.

Wendell mulled things over in his mind. He would never have imagined that Billy would turn on him, or the family that took him in, but he'd seen Billy slowly change, like the phases of the moon from new to full. Wendell never wanted to kill anyone; that's why he planned the robberies with such care. He understood Billy shooting the guard. The guard pulled on him. But the girl. The sight of her, leg near blown off lying on the sidewalk, haunted him.

Maybe it's time to quit, he thought. He entertained that thought for a moment, then clenched his fists hard enough to crack walnuts. No. I can't quit yet. There's one more bank to rob.

Wendell stood and started for the house.

"So how much have we got now?" It was a question Carlene asked often, and Arvin had always found it amusing, until today. He ignored her.

"Arvin," her voice notched up a little higher. "How much?"

"Enough."

"Enough money?"

"No, enough out of you. Shut up."

"Don't you talk to me like that. I'll tell Ernest and —"

The argument was abruptly cut off by Wendell's appearance in the doorway. "Call everybody together. We have to talk."

BIGGS, IOWA

The plan was a hard sell to Payden, but the Deputy Director slowly came around to the agents' reasoning. "And how long do you propose to sit on this bank like a mother hen? The Guthries have gone as long as six weeks between robberies. I can't devote resources for that long a time."

"I understand, sir," Fowler said. "But I'm sure, as careful as the Guthries seem to be, that they wouldn't walk into a bank cold. They'd case it first. One agent in place could watch for suspicious activity. If he sees good reason, a task force in liaison with the Sheriff and the Highway Patrol could be ready to go."

Payden was silent for a while. He finally nodded and said, "All right, Fowler, I'll trust your judgment, but one agent may not be enough. Take Kendall with you. That will still leave me with a full staff."

"Thank you, sir."

As they left the office, Shaw said, "I don't know how you persuaded the Boss so quickly. We usually get the automatic 'no' at least twice before he agrees to anything that isn't his idea."

"Ever hear Mark Twain's definition of an 'expert?'"

Shaw shook his head. "Nope. How's it go?"

"Anyone from more than fifty miles away."

WESTERN KANSAS

"It's time we stop." The Guthrie clan sat around the battered table in the farmhouse kitchen. Wendell looked from face to face, gauging the responses. "This has turned into something none of us ever intended."

"But it was Billy's fault," Duane said. "And he's gone. Isn't he?"

Wendell nodded slowly. "Yes. He's gone."

"You killed him."

"I didn't want to. I told him he was out, and he pulled on me." He raised his head and stared at Duane. "I don't have to justify myself to you, Duane, or any of you."

Wendell reached behind him and pulled his automatic from beneath his shirt. He thumbed back the hammer, set it in the middle of the table and sat back, his arms folded. "Any of you think I was wrong, take it and shoot me now." His hard stare swept the table. No one moved. "Billy forgot why we're on this road. Maybe you have too."

"But if we quit, then you're forgetting too," Arvin said. "We started this war as payback for Daddy and Mama. Are we walking away from that?"

"No," Wendell said, "I haven't forgotten and that's why I say we quit — after we do one last job."

"Fillburn," Arvin said.

Wendell nodded emphatically. "Fillburn. And then we split up the money and go our ways." He looked up at Carlene and Ernest. "Are you with us?"

The pair looked at each other, and Ernest said, "We are."

"I been thinking about this, and here's what we're going to do . . . ."

"Nobody'll mistake this for a bureau car. How's it feel?" Fowler asked. He and Kendall were on the road to Fillburn. Kendall was driving the new cream-colored Oldsmobile F-37 sedan that Payden had commandeered from a local dealer. It sported white wall tires and twin spares set in the front fenders. Fowler had requested a car that wasn't immediately identifiable as one from the Bureau fleet, and Payden had come through.

More important than the looks, it had a straight-eight engine that would serve them well if it came to a chase.

"The steering's a little tight, but I like the big tires; more rubber on the road for stopping and for tight turns." He switched off the crackling two-way radio the mechanics had installed and turned on the car radio. In a minute, big band music poured from the dashboard speaker. "That's more like it. Let's see what she'll do." Kendall pressed the accelerator and the speedometer jumped from sixty miles an hour to eighty, to ninety, and to a hundred. Outside, the wheat blurred from individual stalks to a tawny blur.

They came up fast on a hay wagon. Kendall whipped the wheel left and right and swept past the startled farmer driving the tractor. Two miles further and they could see nothing in either lane. "Okay, hold on." Kendall simultaneously stomped the clutch, tugged at the emergency brake and whipped the steering wheel hard left. The car slid broadside into a bootlegger's street turn. Kendall yanked the wheel into the skid, and the rear end whipped back into the lane. He accelerated again, then stood on the brake, and the car screeched to a long halt. "Not bad."

Fowler nodded. "Seems it'll do the job. If it comes to a chase, you drive."

"Wouldn't have it any other way."

FILLBURN, KANSAS

Fillburn Kansas looked eerily like Biggs, Iowa; a dusty main street for five blocks, a rail depot, and one solitary traffic light to make sure people were forced to stop long enough to at least acknowledge the town's existence. A mile out of town in any direction, the highways became paved trenches between walls of wheat.

The First National Bank of Kansas, Fillburn Branch was in the center of Main Street between a dress shop and a hardware store. Outside the bank, two old men basked in the sun on a bench. A few cars and farm trucks rolled through town. At the end of the block across the street, Fowler spotted a buff brick building with a sign that said Municipal Building.

Kendall parked across the street and he and Fowler got out of the Oldsmobile. The temperature was climbing along with the sun, but both wore their suit coats to cover their guns.

The street wasn't busy. About half of the parking spaces were filed with cars and pickup trucks, many of them rusted and held together with bailing wire. The Depression may be just about over, Fowler thought, but the news hasn't hit Kansas yet.

The Sheriff's office was at the back of the ground floor of the Municipal Building. They stepped into the anteroom to find a paunchy deputy up to his jowls in an egg salad sandwich. He set it down on its waxed paper wrapper and gulped down his bite and smiled broadly. "Howdy. I'm Deputy Warren Jeffries. What can I do for you?"

Fowler showed his badge. "I'm FBI Agent Daniel Fowler, and this is Agent Lawrence Kendall. We'd like to see Sheriff Beck."

The deputy rose from his chair, wiping his hands on a napkin. "I'll tell

Alvin you're here."

He disappeared through a pebbled glass door into an inner office.

"Looks like a slow day," Kendall said. He pointed to the end of the room where a pair of holding cells stood empty.

"But they're ready in case that changes." A rack of rifles, riot guns and double barreled shotguns, hung on the wall just inside the door.

The inner office door opened and a rangy, sandy haired man in a khaki uniform like Jeffries' stepped out. His nose had been broken more than once, it seemed, and the ridge of scar tissue along his sunburned brow said ex-pug. The scars across his knuckles when he held out his hand to shake said brawler.

"I'm Alvin Beck. Which one of you is Agent Fowler?"

"That would be me." Fowler shook hands with Beck and felt the power in the Sheriff's grip. "Good to meet you, Sheriff. This is Agent Larry Kendall."

"I figured you'd be by before too long."

Fowler nodded. "Can we step in your office?"

"Sure thing."

Beck's office was small and cramped with a desk and three chairs. The window was open giving a scenic view of the brick wall across the alley. He turned a table top fan to share the breeze with his visitors. "Hot day," Beck said, nodding at the crescents of sweat forming in his armpits.

"Yeah," Kendall said. "Fry bacon on the sidewalk."

Beck chuckled. "So, I guess you're still looking for the Guthries."

"We have reason to think they may be headed this way."

"Do tell. Why's that?"

For the next half hour, Fowler detailed his theory to the Sheriff, who sat quietly and listened, occasionally asking pertinent questions. When they got to the liaison with the Highway Patrol, Beck snorted. "Hell, they only have thirty cars and four motorcycles for the whole state. They don't have two way radios. They transmit their information through WIBW in Topeka. I don't know how much help they could be. As for local police, there's no official department, just three elected constables."

"We're thinking roadblocks and maybe back up support if we get the Guthries cornered."

"If they come here at all."

"We have a pretty good hunch they will."

"I have four deputies. We'll give you all the support we can, but as for the Highway Patrol, you'll have to talk with Commander Allen."

"Deputy Director Payden is handling that end."

"Well, I hope he isn't disappointed."

"The Bureau appreciates your cooperation, Sheriff. And one other thing —"

"What's that?"

"Our success depends on surprise. If the Guthries think the Bureau is nosing around Fillburn, they won't show their faces. Please tell your deputies to not mention that we're in town."

"No problem. Things've been pretty dull around here. I guess that's about to change."

"It could be a blessing either way."

The First National Bank had a revolving door at the main entrance, and a guard posted just inside. "I guess one guard is enough for the traffic this place sees."

"Remember the Fayette Bank in Pennsylvania? They had snipers in coverts in the dome of the main room on the days when the mine payrolls came in."

"Those days are over."

"Yeah, the last I heard, Frick and Carnegie shut down the mines, picked up all the marbles and left all those immigrant workers stranded. Kinda like the dust bowl farmers."

The bank was testimony to boom times gone bust; marble counters and brass teller cages. The ceiling featured a dome with stained glass panels. A hardwood divider separated the main lobby from the desks of the clerks and officers. But one of the white marble counters was cracked, the brass was tarnished, and overhead, a few of the hand-sized panes of colored glass were missing, replaced with pieces of wood. Money may be coming in, but the bank had felt the pinch the same as everyone else.

Fowler pushed the swing gate aside and walked back to the desk area. A young man in a suit stood up behind a desk with the name plate James Holdorf, Cashier and hurried over. "Can I help you gentlemen?"

Fowler said quietly, "We need to speak to your boss without attracting any undue attention." Dan opened his I.D. folder and showed Holdorf his badge. The cashier's eyes widened. "And we need to speak with him now."

Holdorf nodded, a little too quickly for confidence. "Certainly. Come with me." He led them through the cluster of desks to an office door with Robert Albright, President painted on it in gold leaf. He rapped on the door, and a husky voice said, "Who is it?"

"It's Holdorf, sir. There are men here to see you," he hesitated, "from the FBI."

"What?"

Kendall pushed past Holdorf and through the door with Fowler behind him. "I'm Special Agent Lawrence Kendall of the Federal Bureau of Investigation. This is my partner Special Agent Daniel Fowler.

Albright was a big man even sitting in his high backed desk chair. He was in a vest and white shirt, his tie neatly knotted at the collar. His coat hung on a valet chair in the corner. His round face was lightly filmed with sweat. An accounting ledger was spread open on the blotter of his desk.

Albright was not impressed. His ego wouldn't permit it. "Beck told me you'd be along eventually. Have a seat." Fowler and Kendall looked at each other, and each took a chair. "Holdorf, you'll excuse us please." Holdorf nodded nervously. "And keep your mouth shut. Not a word, understood?"

Again the nervous nod. "Yes, sir."

The door closed, and Albright took a long time carefully lighting a cigar. "Beck says you think the Guthrie gang is going to rob this bank."

"We think that's a very high probability," Fowler said. "After all, the Guthrie family has a pretty heavy grudge against you and your bank. Their Father was killed while you were foreclosing on the family farm."

"Samson Guthrie." Albright blew a cloud of smoke. "The drunken bastard came running at me with a shotgun. I didn't tell the deputies to shoot."

"No, said Kendall, "but you took three of them with you. You were expecting trouble."

Albright's face darkened. "I'm not on trial here, fellow. It's not my fault those dust eaters couldn't pay their mortgage."

Kendall's face darkened to match. "No, but you —"

Fowler cut him off. "Mister Albright, if, as we believe, the Guthries have targeted this bank, it will give us an opportunity to stop them once and for all. The Bureau needs your cooperation."

"I'll cooperate," the banker said. "There's nothing I'd like better than to see those degenerates behind bars, or at the end of a rope."

Larry opened his mouth to speak and Fowler kicked his foot. "We appreciate that, Mister Albright. We are putting a plan together and we will meet with you, Sheriff Beck, and the Highway Patrol to discuss the details." He rose and Kendall followed his lead.

As they reached the door, Albright said, "And Fowler —" The agents turned. "Don't think for a moment that I'm afraid of those creatures." He opened his desk drawer, drew out a Police Special .38, and set it on his desk blotter. If they come through that door, I'll shoot every one of them I see."

"We'd rather no one be shot. Mister Albright," Fowler said. "My advice is to let us handle this and maybe no one will be hurt."

"Albright's going to be a problem," Larry said as they crossed the street. "I hope not."

He opened his desk drawer, drew out a Police Special .38...

"His attitude was pretty clear. He didn't say one word about the safety of his employees."

"I tried to be diplomatic," Fowler said. "I was afraid you were going to climb over his desk and punch him in the teeth."

"Or vice-versa." Kendall snorted. "Ever meet somebody you just can't tolerate from the very start?"

"I think Beck may be helpful to bring him in line."

"Did you see the photos on the wall behind his desk? Besides him with the local Rotary Club, I saw him with the Governor, him with Senator Cleary; all that's missing is one with Eleanor Roosevelt. I hope he doesn't pick up the phone and throw his weight around, try to run things."

"I have an idea how to handle that." He looked up and down the street. "Let's see where we can get some lunch. My stomach's digesting itself."

They met with Beck, Captain Grover Woods from the Kansas Highway Patrol and Albright in Beck's office. Take Albright away from his turf, off his throne, Fowler thought, and he won't think he's got so much clout. Captain Woods was in his late forties, and as fit as Jim Thorpe. That combined with his blunt features and close cropped hair made him look like Mob enforcers Fowler had run into on occasion.

"Let's start this off with the idea that we all have the same goal in mind," Beck said.

"And what goal is that?" Albright said.

"You'll find out if you shut your trap and listen, Bob. Agent Fowler and Agent Kendall are the experts, so let them talk."

"Sheriff Beck is right, Fowler said. "We have the same goal, and I want that to be clear to everyone." He looked pointedly at Albright, Beck, and Woods in turn. "We want to apprehend the Guthrie gang, and we want to do it without the situation turning into another Biggs-style shootout. The less gunplay the better, wouldn't you agree, Captain Woods?"

Woods nodded. "I don't want to see anyone killed, officers, bystanders, anyone. And if we can take the Guthries alive, we should. I don't want this to turn into the O.K. Corral."

"Sheriff Beck?"

"Yeah, I agree. I don't want anybody killed on my watch."

Fowler intentionally ignored Albright. "Ideally, the Bureau will find the gang and apprehend them before they ever pull the job, but if they make a play, we have to be ready."

"Well, if you see them, why not shoot them on sight?" Albright said.

Fowler slapped a file folder on Beck's desk. He snarled, "That's why." He flipped the folder open and slid the photo of Annie Tyler on the desk in front of the banker. "And that." He put the picture of George Smith, dead on the sidewalk, beside it. "And that." He added the stark photo shot through the jagged glass of the police car windshield, the dead officer at the wheel. Albright stared at the pictures. "We don't want a repeat of this in Fillburn."

"There's an extensive search going on in western Kansas now," Kendall said, "and if we find the Guthries first, they'll never come here at all, but in the meantime, we have a plan of surveillance in mind. Their *modus operandi,* like most stick-up artists, includes casing a bank in advance, and if they hold to it, one of them will show up sooner or later. Agent Fowler and I will be in the lobby working undercover, and we should be able to spot whoever comes in."

"So that's your plan?" Albright snapped. "Just sit around and wait for them to rob the bank?"

"I'll have a man watching the building from the outside," said Beck, "so you'll be covered inside and out. And if anything pops, we'll call you right away," he said to Grover.

"I have the whole state to maintain," the Captain said, "but I'll have the patrols in this quarter on alert."

"And Agent Kendall and I will be in the bank from open to close," Fowler said, "And I must ask that your employees not be told why we're in place. People talk, and if word gets out, it may scare the Guthries away and we'll never catch them."

"All right," Albright said. "I'll keep it quiet."

"Then starting tomorrow, Agent Kendall and I will be in place. Let's hope the dragnet finds the Guthries and we don't have to deal with a robbery."

WESTERN KANSAS

Just after sunset, Arvin blew the horn as he rolled the black Chrysler Airstream into the front yard of the farmhouse. Everyone came outside. As they did, Duane pulled in behind him in the flivver.

"What do you think? He said as he stepped out of the car.

"It's a beauty," Carlene said. She turned to Ernest. "Can we keep it after the job?"

"Sis, I'll buy us one when this is all over. Or a Cadillac if you want it."

"Where'd you steal it?" Wendell said.

"In the next state." He wiped the dust from the fender. She's got an L-head eight gives a hundred and five horses."

"It'll do. Have it ready for tomorrow." Wendell turned around and went back into the house.

"Wendell," said Arvin, "Tomorrow? Aren't we going to case the bank first, like all the others?"

"I've seen it enough times."

FILLBURN, KANSAS JULY 16

The original plan was for Fowler and Kendall to pose as bank examiners and sit at a desk beside the teller area, but they decided finally that they were better off to cover the lobby with one at a desk and one at a teller's window. They flipped a coin and Fowler got the teller's cage. Tom Weldon, one of Beck's deputies posed as a guard just inside the door.

"And how would you like that, Ma'am?" Fowler said, opening the cash drawer under the teller's window. It was nearly noon, and the lobby was almost empty.

"I'd like it all in five dollar bills, please." The elderly lady on the other side of the teller's cage smiled benignly. "I have four grandchildren, and if you would, please give me nice new ones. I hate to give them old rumpled bills."

"Yes, ma'am." He reached into the drawer and his fingers closed on the butt of his .45 automatic. His eye followed Duane Guthrie as the thug walked through the revolving door. He was wearing a raincoat on a sunny day. No subtlety, no subterfuge.

Fowler looked to his partner Larry Kendall, who sat nearby at an assistant manager's desk. Kendall nodded tersely and picked up the phone. He had seen him too. The line was open to Sheriff Beck's office. Fowler's hunch had proved right; the Guthries had come for revenge.

Fowler counted out the fives with his left hand, keeping his right on the pistol. Beck's deputy Tom Weldon was looking the wrong way for Fowler to signal him. Dan could feel a bead of sweat run between his shoulder blades and down his back. Look past him, not at him. "Five, ten, fifteen, twenty. There you are ma'am. Have a nice day."

Fowler's eye kept twitching toward the entrance. Duane stopped at a customer counter as if he were filling out a deposit slip. The door turned and Wendell and Ernest stepped inside.

"Oh, and would you please look up my Christmas Club balance for me?"

"Uh, ma'am, I think you should —"

Wendell swept open his coat and swung a sawed-off twelve-gauge Remington pump on a strap, catching Weldon full in the face. The deputy went down, and Wendell took his revolver from its holster and jammed it in the waistband of his trousers. He fired a shot at the ceiling with the Remington that boomed like a stick of dynamite, then leveled the shotgun at the startled customers queued at the teller windows. "This is a robbery. Nobody moves, nobody gets hurt." His eyes swept the tellers. "No alarms or I shoot everybody I see."

Duane opened his coat and pulled out a shotgun to match his brother's. Ernest pulled up a Thompson with a straight clip. Duane vaulted the gated divider and nearly fell as he landed in front of Kendall's desk. He aimed the gun at Larry and threw a canvas sack onto it. "You. Fill it up from the drawers, then we're going into the vault."

Larry took the sack in his right hand and held his left one in the air palm forward. "Okay, Mister. I'll do what you say. Just please don't hurt anybody."

He moved toward the teller windows. Fowler was trying to watch all three of the Guthries at the same time. If he made a wrong move, Duane would blow a hole in Larry and take a few other people with him. Larry began taking the cash from the first drawer, and Fowler got an idea. He left his pistol under a sheaf of twenties then took a step backward.

Larry got to the second window. Fowler's was next. Over Duane's shoulder, Fowler saw the barrel of a pistol coming out of the doorway to Albright's office. No, he thought. Don't be stupid. Larry was at Fowler's drawer now, Duane watching his every move. He snarled at Fowler, "Back up, bright eyes." Fowler took two steps back, which put him out of reach of the shotgun, but put him beside a desk he could use for cover.

"Where's Albright?" Wendell shouted.

"Right here, you son of a bitch." Albright stood in his office doorway, pistol in his hand.

Everything happened at once.

A customer in a white suit and a straw boater panicked and tried to run, thrusting his money into his pocket. Wendell saw the movement from the corner of his eye, and thinking he was going for a gun, pulled the trigger. The shotgun blast knocked the man off his feet, leaving him lying on the terrazzo floor with red carnations blooming on his chest.

Albright fired at Wendell and missed him, the slug whanging off a marble cornice.

Duane's eyes twitched toward the gunshot. Larry swung Fowler's automatic from the drawer and put a round in the robber's shoulder. Fowler rolled behind the desk as Duane's shotgun jerked to the right and blew double-aught buckshot through the spot where Fowler had just been standing. He pulled his backup piece from an ankle holster and put two rounds in Duane's forehead. Larry swiveled and crouched behind the counter to fire through the grille of the teller's cage. "FBI! Everyone get down!"

The customers and tellers hit the floor as Ernest cut loose with the Thompson at Albright. The banker pitched over backward as brass spewed from the ejection port and rolled across the polished floor. Then Ernest sent a spray of bullets ricocheting off the marble. People screamed, some from terror and some from catching a stray slug.

Larry fired, and Ernest caught one in the shoulder, but he kept shooting.

Weldon grabbed Wendell around his knees and tried to pull him down. Wendell swung the shotgun toward the deputy and fired. Larry popped up to fire and caught Wendell in the leg.

Outside, Beck ran for the revolving door, a riot gun in his hands. "Ma'am, get down!" Beck shouted as he ran past Carlene, who ducked behind a parked car, pulled a revolver from her purse, and shot him in the back. Beck's body fell half in and half out of the revolving door, blocking it.

Ernest fired another burst, and Larry went down. "The money!" Ernest shouted. "Get the money!"

"Money, hell, you fool!" Wendell shouted back. "Run!" He limped to the revolving door and finding it jammed, blew out the glass with his shotgun. He stepped through the jagged pane over Beck's body. Ernest laid down another spray of fire for cover and followed Wendell.

Fowler grabbed Duane's shotgun and dived over the divider, rolling to his feet as he hit and running toward the entrance. He fired through the entranceway, but Ernest was out and around the corner.

Ernest and Wendell hit the sidewalk and within two seconds, Arvin rolled up in the Chrysler. The deputy across the street fired from behind a parked truck and blew out a back window. Arvin stuck a pistol out his window and fired a half dozen shots to cover for Wendell and Ernest.

They jumped into the car and Carlene clambered in the back, losing a shoe.

Arvin said, "Where's Duane?"

Wendell shouted, "He's dead! Go! Go!"

Arvin cracked the gas and the tires squealed as he sped away from the curb.

Fowler heard sirens coming outside. He ran back to the teller cages, where Larry was sitting up, propped against a desk. His shirt was red with blood and pink froth bubbled from a hole in his chest.

Fowler wadded his handkerchief and pressed it against Larry's wound.

"Did you get them?"

"Don't try to talk." Fowler loosened Larry's tie. "Don't worry. We'll get them."

Uniformed deputies were climbing through the shattered door.

Larry let out a wet, ragged cough. "Damn it. Ruined my best suit."

"Shut up and save your breath. The ambulance'll be here soon."

He walked around the divider and saw the little old woman he'd waited on moments before. She was crouched on her hands and knees, head between her elbows. "It's over ma'am. You're safe now."

She raised her head and gave Fowler a glassy-eyed stare. "Wait 'til I tell my grandchildren."

Fowler grabbed one of the deputies by the arm. "Did they get away?"

"Yeah. They headed north in a black sedan, Chrysler, I think."

Fowler dashed out the door to the Oldsmobile parked at the curb. He stepped on the starter and the big engine rumbled to life. As he sped down Main Street and into the wheat-lined corridor, he switched on the two way radio. "Wilcox, Fowler. Do you read? Over."

Wilcox's voice was scratchy from static. "I read you, Fowler. Is the situation hot?"

"It is. The suspects are headed north on County Road 302 in a black sedan, likely a Chrysler."

"On our way."

Ahead, the road lay as straight as the barrel of a gun. The speedometer needle climbed steadily and the Oldsmobile shot down the road like a Fourth of July rocket. In the distance, Fowler saw a dark shape on the horizon. This time they wouldn't escape. He coaxed a little more from the engine, and the speedometer needle pushed against the top end.

COUNTY ROAD 302

"Oh, my God," Carlene said. "Duane's dead?"

"Yeah," Wendell said through clenched teeth as he pulled his handkerchief tight around his leg. The shot missed his artery, but the blood flow was steady. "But so is that bastard Albright. I only regret that I didn't shoot him myself."

"What went wrong?" Arvin said.

"Cops in the bank, FBI; I don't know how they knew, but they were ready for us."

"What do we do now?"

"Follow the plan. Drive."

Carlene looked out the rear windshield. "I see a car behind us. Way back."

Ernest climbed onto the seat on his knees to look for himself. "He's too far back to see who it is, but it's not one of those silver top Highway Patrol cars."

"Slow down," Wendell said.

"What?"

"Let him get closer. Ernest can shoot him from the back window."

Arvin took a deep breath and eased off the accelerator, the Chrysler slowed to eighty. "Is he gaining?"

"Yeah," Ernest said. "In a minute he'll be right behind us." He used the butt of the Thompson to punch out the glass. "Let him come. I'll be ready."

A shadow swept over the hood of the car. "What the hell?" Arvin said, as he leaned forward to peer upward through the windshield. Wendell leaned out his window and saw a red and yellow biplane circling to the east. "It's a god damned airplane."

The plane circled behind them and out of sight. The chase car was gaining on the Chrysler. Arvin looked in the side mirror and saw the cream colored sedan closing on them. Another thirty seconds, and Ernest would take care of him.

They heard the drone of an engine, and the red and yellow biplane swooped six feet over the car. It followed the road ahead of the Chrysler, and a thick white cloud poured from its tail section.

Everyone choked at the white crop dust that poured through the open windows. Arvin's eyes teared up and he couldn't see to steer. The Chrysler veered off the road and dove into the waving wheat. The car plowed through about a hundred feet before it hit a disc harrow hidden by the stalks and flipped sideways. It rolled once and the driver's door flew open. Arvin was halfway out as the car rolled again, slamming the door on his neck, and coming to rest on its roof.

Carlene was shrieking, and Wendell shouted, "Shut up!" He crawled, coughing, through his window and walked around the wreck. Arvin lay beside the car, his head turned nearly backwards.

"Help me," Carlene shouted. Ernest's hurt." Wendell bent over and looked through the window. Ernest was gritting his teeth and clutching his shoulder. "I think my collarbone's broken."

Wendell yanked the back door open with the grating sound of a sardine lid. "Give me your arm." Wendell took Ernest by the wrist with both hands and dragged him out of the back. Ernest screamed, and Carlene shouted, "You're killing him!"

Wendell reached in to retrieve the Thompson. He pulled Ernest roughly to his feet. "Come on," Wendell said, looking at the path through the wheat. "We have to get away from here."

"To where?" Carlene said.

"We'll hide in the wheat 'til it gets dark. Help me with him." Wendell put a shoulder in Ernest's armpit and started dragging him away from the wreck. Carlene took off running and left Wendell to the chore. He'd gotten about four steps when he heard a muffled voice say, "Freeze. FBI."

Wendell turned to see Fowler in a gas mask pointing a revolver at him. Wendell swung the machine gun one-handed, and fired a spray of bullets. Fowler hit the ground just in time. Wendell pulled the trigger again, and nothing happened. The magazine was empty. He still had Weldon's revolver in his waistband. He pulled it, but before he could fire, Fowler put two rounds in his chest.

Fowler stood and pulled the mask over his head. He kicked the pistol away from Wendell's dead hand. Ernest groaned. He had passed out from the pain and was just coming around. Fowler crouched beside him to do a quick frisk for weapons. A shrill voice made him turn his head.

"It's not fair! We almost had it made! You ruined everything!" Carlene stood over him sobbing, both hands aiming the pistol from her handbag at his head. "It's not fair!"

"Drop it." Wilcox stepped from the wheat, his automatic pointed at her.

"Aaaugh!" Carlene snarled and whirled, wild eyed, to shoot her new antagonist. Wilcox's gun boomed, and the pistol flew from her grip in a spray of blood and bone. She fell to her knees, staring at her ruined hands and wailing.

"Where did you come from?"

"Barnes put his plane down on the highway. I just followed the trail through the field."

"That was some pretty fancy shooting, Dean."

"Hell, I was aiming at her head."

FILLBURN, KANSAS JULY 17

Larry Kendall's hospital bed was cranked up about thirty degrees, and a pretty red-haired nurse was plumping his pillow. "Hello, Dan," he said. "Say hello to Maggie. Maggie, this is my partner, Dan Fowler." His chest was crisscrossed with bandages, and his left arm was taped to it, so Fowler opened the newspaper and held it to let Larry read the headline: FBI NABS GUTHRIE GANG IN CHASE. Below it was the sub head: DEPUTY DIRECTOR PRAISES LAW ENFORCEMENT LIAISON.

Kendall laughed then winced at the pain. "From what I hear, the headline should be FBI *AGENT* NABS GUTHRIE GANG. But Payden would grab the credit, wouldn't he?"

"Rank has its privileges. It doesn't matter. I'm just glad we won that one."

"Me too. How's Beck?"

"At least as sore as you are, but he'll heal."

"Too bad Weldon didn't make it."

"Fortunes of war. By the way, we were right about the gang's hideouts. They were all in Kansas and about where we figured they were. We found getaway cars and caches of food and ammo, but we still haven't found the money. Sooner or later we will. Wilcox and Shaw'll probably be able squeeze it out of the Veatch twins."

"When do you fly back to D.C.?"

"Tomorrow morning."

"Give the Director my regards."

Maggie brought a basin of water and a towel. "Time for your sponge bath, Larry."

As she reached to pull the curtain around the bed, Fowler said. "I'll tell him I left you in good hands."

THE END

Family Afoul: author's notes

Ialways feel a little wary when I write fiction with other people's characters, but once I got rolling with a story line, I felt comfortable with Dan Fowler, G-Man. People often tell me that my stories are an escape for the reader but I believe they are as much an escape for me as I write them. Dan Fowler is a figure from the golden era of investigation before computer databases, the internet, DNA testing, drones, cell phones, surveillance cameras, and many other technical marvels that make being an investigator less a matter of wit and pluck than reliance on the genie of modern technology.

The FBI had only been using fingerprinting (the "Ident" system) for ten years, and its Criminology Laboratory officially opened in 1932, so forensic science was still new, and investigations were conducted largely the old way: shoe leather and blackjacks.

The Thirties in the Midwest still had a lot of the Old West clinging to it, and local and state law enforcement was playing catch-up with the gangster era. The Iowa Highway patrol began in 1935 with fifty officers and the Kansas Highway patrol in 1937 had 31 automobiles, none of which had two-way radios or even cherry-top roof beacons. In such a scenario, agents like Dan Fowler are analogous to Old West Marshals or Texas Rangers, tough professionals who ride in and deal with the bad guys.

The idea of bank robbers who are not in it simply for the money or the glory appealed to me. Revenge on The Bank as an abstract entity for the loss of the family farm and family members appealed to me as motivation, especially for the eldest of the Guthrie clan, and it supported the internal logic of the actions the gang takes through the story.

I had a lot of fun writing "Family Afoul," and in portraying Dan Fowler as a working G-Man. I hope you all have as much fun reading it.

FRED ADAMS, JR. is a retired Penn State University English Professor who spends his days writing pulp fiction and his nights working as a singer-songwriter. His Sam Dunne novel *Dead Man's Melody* was nominated as Pulp Novel of the Year in 2017's Pulp Factory Awards, and his Smith Brothers novel *The Eye of Quang-Chi* was nominated for the same award in 2018. His titles include *Hitwolf* 1 and 2, *Six Gun Terrors* vols. 1, 2, and 3, and *C.O. Jones: Mobsters and Monsters, Skinners,* and *The Damned and the Doomed.* His original Sherlock Holmes anthology *The Affair of the Chronic Argonaut* was recently published by Pro Se Press. Forthcoming titles from

Airship 27 include *C.O. Jones: Home Front*, *Six Gun Terrors 4: The Town Killers*, a Sam Dunne Mystery, *Blood is the New Black*, and *Holster Full of Death*, a Dead Sheriff novel. He lives in Mount Pleasant, Pennsylvania in "perpetual terror of boredom."

Visit Fred's website at http://drphreddee.com/author